FURY OF
AFFLICTION

A
DRAGONFURY
COLLECTION

COREENE
CALLAHAN

OLIVER HEBER BOOKS

THE DRAGON, THE MAN, AND THE ARMCHAIR

A DRAGONFURY SHORT STORY

1

BLACK DIAMOND LAIR—THE HUB

Sometimes the only thing that helped was hitting something hard. Leaning into the age-old truth, Sloan slammed his fists into the punching bag. Left jab. Right cross. Uppercut. Sweat rolling down his spine, he pivoted into a high kick.

His foot struck black leather.

The heavy bag swung.

Thick chains jerked.

The clank rippled across the gym, bouncing off cinder-block walls only to boomerang back toward him. Rage swam in the sound. In each strike. Carving into him like a blade, making him bleed a little more with every heartbeat. His knuckles hurt. His muscles ached. His mind screamed. And yet, he couldn't stop. Refused to deny the need, ignoring the clock as one hour rounded into two, and he pummelled his imaginary opponent.

He didn't need a face...or a name. The target didn't matter. Pain called the play, folding the memory into a loop inside his head. Relentless in pursuit. Ruthless in intensity. Inescapable, the same way it always was this time of year.

Baring his teeth, he hammered the bag again. Leather groaned then cratered. Stitches popped. The seam split wide-open. Saw dust and stuffing flew in all directions. As the mess spilled onto the narrowed-planked floor, he hit pause on the brutal onslaught to scowl at the fist-sized hole.

"Shit."

Ruined.

He'd *ruined* the only heavy bag in the gym. Something his brothers-in-arms used often. All in an effort to assuage his temper. He wanted to ask himself why he bothered, but knew it didn't matter. Year after year, he suffered just the same. Finding an outlet never helped. Nothing he tried ever did. No matter how hard he worked out—or slammed his fists into shit—the rage boiling beneath his surface remained. Always there. Never satisfied. Which meant…

He needed to stop.

Right now.

Before his dragon half took control. Before the heavy weave of his earth magic boiled over. Before he unleashed a seismic tremor so devastating it cracked granite and shook his packmates awake from where he stood seven stories underground.

None of the warriors he lived with would be happy with the shake-up. All of them would get in his face about it. Demand to know what was bothering him. Sit him down. Force him to explain and relive what he wanted to let go, but knew he never would.

With a muffled curse, Sloan spun on his heel. Swiping the file folder he'd abandoned earlier on an exercise bench, he strode out of the weight room and into the gymnasium. The rubber soles of his boxing shoes squeaked across hardwood. The scent of floor wax and sweat hit him. Kicking a basketball out of his way, he snarled and started for the exit.

Full of fury, magic frothed out in front of him.

Harnessing the power, he murmured his wishes. Hinges hissed. Reinforced steel panels whipped open. A satisfying clang reverberated as metal handles slammed into granite walls. Dust puffed up. The doors whipped back in his direction. Pace steady, strides even, he avoided the backlash and stalked into the hallway. Wide double doors slammed behind him. The echoing violence of his exit quieted. His footfalls picked up the slack, thumping along the corridor as he pivoted toward his computer lab.

Same view, different day. Wide hallway with twelve-foot ceilings. Round lights embedded in polished concrete floors throwing V-shaped splashes up scarred, white-washed walls carved from solid granite.

Right now, the lights were dimmed down.

Later, when his brothers-in-arms rolled out bed to start the day, soft illumination would power into a bright glow, absorbing the energy his packmates threw off like supernovas. Par for the course with so many magically gifted males inside Black Diamond.

With the addition of Azrad, Kilmar and Terranon, the Nightfury pack had gone from elite heavy-weights to a Dragonkind powerhouse. As individuals, all three warriors packed a serious punch. Combined, the trio became poster boys for brutality, delivering the kind of ferocity smart males avoided if they wanted to stay alive.

Blood sport.

Exactly want he needed right now.

Sparring with Azrad would improve his mood. Kilmar would no doubt be a good choice too. And Terranon? He didn't know the warrior well, but the Aussie seemed like a male who gave worse than he got, making him an ideal target in Sloan's current state of mind. Going twenty rounds would help him forget what sat inside his computer lab.

Sloan growled under his breath.

Goddamn Daimler.

The Numbai needed to stop before Sloan lost his mind. Every time the Nightfury go-to guy pulled this kind of shit, the scabbed-over wound inside him reopened, sending him careening down memory lane. A place Sloan never enjoyed visiting. But Daimler—in typical Numbai fashion—refused to relent. He kept hoping Sloan would change his mind and get rid of his chair.

The purple monstrosity.

The eyesore.

The thing fucking up the aesthetic in the Hub according to Daimler and everyone else who called Black Diamond home.

Fighting to find his center, Sloan drew a deep breath and kept walking. Toward sanity. Toward certainty. Toward his super computer and the one place guaranteed to quiet the chaotic clang inside his head.

Magic slithering through his veins, he stopped on the Hub's threshold. Prickles ghosted down his spine. Cool air stirred. His night vision sparked, lighting up dark corners, giving him the lay of the land.

Nothing and nobody. All quiet, for a freaking change.

Surrounded by the buzz of electricity, co-cooned in stillness, Sloan reached for calm. He closed his eyes, then took another deep breath. The silence hit him like a body shot. He absorbed the blow. Gladly. With relish. Aware the solitude wouldn't last long.

It never did inside the lair, but after too many nights of non-stop action, he needed respite from the chatter. From all the good-natured threats his brothers tossed around like live hand grenades every time the pack of lunatics invaded the Hub, kicked back and stayed awhile.

With a sigh, Sloan flicked his wrist. The file folder he carried sailed toward the com-center. Red cardstock hit the target, spilling documents across the desktop as he moved deeper into the room. His keyboard shimmied sideways. Motion sensors activated. The wall-mounted monitors flipped on as his system powered up.

Computer code scrolled across multiple screens.

Gaze moving over the information, he shoved the gaming chair Daimler deemed good enough for him to sit his ass in out of the way. Rubber wheels hissed across smooth concrete. Black leather with red racing strips slammed into the conference table. The stupid thing skittered sideways, then spun into the corner as he palmed the back of his own chair. The one he refused to give up. The one he *couldn't* give up.

Beat-to-shit from loads of wear and tear, the wide bucket seat spun in his direction. Worn white in spots, purple leather flashed in the lowlight. Rusty metal hinges squawked.

Sloan shook his head.

He hadn't meant for it to become a *thing*. Why everyone kept giving him shit about it was a question he wanted to ignore. Usually *ignored*. Excelled at *ignoring*. An excellent strategy given his packmates threw shade better than a pack of professional hecklers, so...

Yeah.

Absolutely.

Ignoring the idiotic opinions tossed his way on a regular basis worked better than the alternative— allowing his packmates to get under his skin.

He'd perfected the skill of not-giving-a-shit-what-anyone-thought over the years. Or so, he'd believed...until his ability to deflect began to unravel three weeks ago. The day he met Theodora, and she preceded to rock his world.

Without effort, his mate cut through his defenses. Bonding with his dragon half. Forcing him out of self-imposed isolation. Becoming the light in his darkness the instant he touched her, and she accepted him as her male.

Sloan's mouth curved.

Goddess, his female. She was so much more than he expected. And after witnessing his pack-mates claim their chosen females, he'd expected a lot. Theodora made a mockery of his expectations. Outspoken and wise. Brilliant and beautiful. Loving and patient. She was exceptional in every way, turning him inside out without even trying. A blessing. A dream come true. A gift Sloan knew he didn't deserve, but accepted without hesitation.

Selfish, maybe, but he didn't care.

Theodora grounded him in ways he found im-possible to quantify. Which meant he shouldn't be in the Hub. Not right now. A smart male knew where to go when he needed calm and under-standing—straight into the arms of his mate. No delay. And yet, not wanting to burden her, he shied away, protecting her from the truth, shielding her from the fallout.

Frowning at his computer, Sloan shook his head. It was madness. Pure ego fueled by fear. A hard turn away from vulnerability toward control. Or at least, the illusion of it.

Theodora wanted him to let go, to trust her enough to turn and face his past. She longed to help him find peace, which made his exit from the bed chamber he shared with her idiotic. It was worse than self-serving. It was complete cow-ardice. He frowned. Not that it mattered. Labeling what drove him into the gym while everyone else slept wouldn't fix the problem. Nothing would ex-cept, maybe…

Sloan sighed.

What in the hell was he doing?

He needed to shift course, return to the green-house and the bed he shared with his female. Should, even now, be holding her while she dreamed, instead of staring at computer screens, struggling to stay even on his own.

Old habits, however, died hard.

And some battles a male must fight on his own.

He was too restless to sleep. Most days, while in the throes of excess energy, he burned off the tension by making love to Theodora. But after he'd kept her up all morning, his mate needed sleep more than she needed pleasure. Violet, their three-year old daughter, would be up soon, so—

Better to suffer alone than exhaust his female.

Typing a correction into a line of code, Sloan watched the screen, then huffed in annoyance. Change never came easy. He preferred smooth, embraced steady, avoiding emotional instability as much as possible. With Theodora, however, the need to pivot became imperative. He must adjust to his new normal, let her all the way in, no matter how uncomfortable the shift.

He owed his mate everything. All of him, every piece, no holds barred or secrets kept. Problem was...

He'd always been a male with secrets. So many, he didn't know where to start. Or how to share all of it without scaring her.

Planting his fist on the desktop, Sloan bowed his head. Goddess help him. The push-pull was tearing him apart. He wanted to tell her. Theodora needed to know, but every time he veered toward honesty his throat closed. Not that his dragon half cared about his struggle.

His beast adored Theodora, opening wide, inviting her in, allowing her to burrow in and settle deep. The idea made him tense. Self-preservation clung to independence and the old ways. His love for Theodora, however, demanded something else. Something new. Something different. Something, if he allowed the vulnerability, would feed her while devouring him.

His dragon embraced the idea.

His human half railed against it.

The dichotomy confused him. Hard lines he never crossed had begun to blur, blending his past with the present, dragging his history into the open, letting the pain he carried out of its cage. Now he didn't feel like himself anymore. He was drowning. Slowly losing himself along with the grip on his volatile nature. Things that never bothered him before, irritated the hell out of him now.

He'd never paid attention to what others thought of him. He was self-contained. A hard shell. An unbreachable castle with a moat full of sharks. Needing another's approval never factored into the equation...until recently. Until Theodora forced him to face an unforgiving truth. One that began and ended with the fact he counted on his packmates. Loved his brothers. Enjoyed being a part of the pack no matter how idiotic the members' antics, leading him to acknowledge an inescapable fact—his packmates' opinion of him mattered.

Which made his withdrawal all the more startling...and insulting.

Like Theodora, his brothers needed him to share. To be honest about his past. To be upfront about the depth of his loss. To allow the pack to carry him through the bad times and encourage him through the good. Which, crazy as it seemed, brought him back to the chair.

His chair.

The *purple monstrosity* everyone hated, and he refused to let go.

His packmates asked about it all the time. So often, Sloan knew he needed to explain, but... fuck. Telling them the truth meant reliving the nightmare. Something he didn't want to do. The reason he kept his chair wasn't anyone's business but his own, and yet the constant questioning bothered him.

He heard the grumbles. Clocked the continued curiosity. Stuffed the hurt down deep every time one of his brothers muttered something derogatory under his breath.

Staring at a gash in the seat cushion, Sloan flexed his hand on the back of his chair. Leather groaned. Frayed stitching popped. He ran his fingertip over a well-worn groove. A scar. One of many his chair had suffered over the years. The familiar feel made bad memories resurface.

His chest tightened.

Deploying an emotional tourniquet, Sloan stemmed the flow and fought through the pain. So his chair was ugly. An eyesore held together by duct tape, mismatched bolts, and cans of WD-40.

The wide, bucket seat wasn't even comfortable anymore, but tossing it in a dumpster would mean throwing away the only thing he had left of—

"Sloan?"

A soft inquiry. Sweet undertones. Her voice. *The voice.* The only one capable of blunting the jagged teeth of his turmoil.

"Honey?"

Prickles ghosted down his spine.

Standing with is back to the door, Sloan closed his eyes. "Theodora. Baby—"

"Why are you here?"

Blanking his expression, he glanced over his shoulder.

Sleepy green eyes met his.

Longing tightened his gut. Pleasure at the sight of her tugged at his heart. Fuck. His female. No one better in the world. No one more adorable either. He would never tire of looking at her. Especially now with a crease from one of his pillows imprinted on her cheek and her long legs on display bcneath the hem an oversized t-shirt. *His t-shirt*, the one she slept in when he didn't have her naked above or beneath him.

Concern in her gaze, she stopped on the threshold. "Sloan—"

"You should be sleeping."

"I'm restless without you."

"I'm—"

"Don't apologize."

"*Mazleiha*—"

"You need to give it to me."

"Theo—"

"You're losing sleep, honey. Now, with everything going on, when you need to stay focused. You can't afford to be tired. It's too dangerous."

She wasn't wrong.

With Rodin and the Archguard gearing up to take down the Nightfury pack—and pack commanders picking sides—Sloan needed to stay sharp. Mistakes cost lives, and unfocused meant dead. Bastian and his brothers were counting on him to sort out the details in order to build a strong coalition of like-minded Dragonkind warriors.

Theodora uncrossed her arms. "Sloan."

"That's off limits."

"Not to me, it isn't." Leveling her chin, she took another step into the room. "I get it all, Sloan. *All of it.* All of you, just like you get all of me. So, the whole silent thing you've got going on is done. No more ignoring the elephant in the room. It's clear you need to talk about it, so you're going to give it to me, and I'm going to take it. Help carry it. Bring you some relief while you face the hard part of healing."

He shook his head. "I'll never heal, baby. Not from a wound like this."

"Okay. Fair enough," she whispered. "But that doesn't mean you need to suffer alone. I can help carry the load, honey. But more, I *need* you to let me."

"Playing dirty."

"No other way with you," she said. "I'd do anything for you, Sloan. Give anything. My beating heart, if necessary."

Fighting the pain, he shook his head.

She gave him a warning look.

He tried to explain. "I don't talk about it, Theo. With anyone."

"I'm not *anyone*."

He frowned. Well, she had him there. Then again, his mate usually did. The bond he shared with her was strong. Unbreakable. So intense, she read him right every single time.

"I'm yours—yeah?"

He nodded. "Yeah."

"And you're mine. What would you do if I was struggling…suffering…and I refused to share the reason with you?"

"Wear you down. Make you talk to me by fucking you into exhaustion."

"Well, I've been doing that all week—"

"Thank the goddess."

"—and you still haven't shared, so now I'm tackling the problem from a different angle," she said, digging in the way she always did when he fell into old patterns. "It's time to tell me, Sloan."

"Don't know if I can."

"You can."

His lips twitched.

Her eyes narrowed.

A standoff. One he was unlikely to win given his mate's stubbornness. Since arriving at Black Diamond, she'd come into her own, personality shining bright, becoming the female she was meant to be, not the one her uncle had forced her to become.

"Sloan."

Unable to find the words, he clenched his teeth.

"His birthday was this week?"

The ball of pain sitting like a bomb in the center of his chest throbbed, threatening to detonate.

"Simeon would be what—twelve now?"

Sloan nodded.

"What day was he born?"

Recall hammered him. The vault he kept locked cracked open, allowing the memory to spill out. Devastation a living, breathing thing, he forced out, "On a Thursday. Full moon. Bright stars in a black sky, twelve years ago yesterday."

"I know how much losing him hurts—"

"It kills, Theo," he rasped. "*Kills.*"

"I see it. I feel it. I hurt when you hurt, but honey, you're already halfway there. You told me his name. You shared that much, so now, take the last step. Let me in on the memory. Give me the rest."

Heart thumping, Sloan drew a ragged breath.

Theodora made a pained sound. "Hope shared something interesting with me the other day. I think it might help."

"What?"

"When Forge gets mired in the past. In the pain, he shares the memory with her without speaking. He downloads the experience like a video file through mind-meld. If it's too much…if you can't find the words…then show me, Sloan. Use our bond to connect and show me. Nothing you do or say will shock me. I know you. I know your heart. I know I can help you find a way through the grief."

So earnest. So understanding. One hundred percent right.

His mate knew how to smooth the way. How to help him even when he didn't know how to help himself. Seeing him suffer hurt her. Instead of turning away, she'd dug in and thrown down by giving him an ultimatum. One that made sense. One his dragon half needed him to honor, so...

Time to decide.

Either he nurtured the bond he shared with Theodora, or he didn't. No middle ground existed. He couldn't have it both ways—sharing when he wanted to, shutting her out when he didn't. Energy-fuse demanded respect. His dragon half was dialed in, waiting for him to pull his head out of his ass and trust Theodora with the truth. With all of him, not just what he felt comfortable giving her. His beast already knew what he kept resisting. In order to do right by her, he must shed old habits and create healthier ones.

Feeling inadequate, not knowing how to meet the moment, he cleared his throat, then raise his hand, palm up, asking her to come to him. "Need you here, *mazleiha.*"

An order. Firm. Determined. Even though, gently said.

Theodora didn't resist. She moved, closing the distance without hesitation.

He sighed in relief as she walked into his arms. Smoothing her hands over his chest, his shoulders and down his back, she pulled him together with her touch, providing what he needed by pressing her cheek to his heart.

Playing with the ends of her hair, he set his mouth against the top of her head. "I don't want to show you."

"Too bad," she whispered, prompting him with a squeeze.

"It isn't pretty."

"And my past is?"

"It's different."

"Why?"

"You're you—brilliant, tenacious and strong. Your heart's aways in the right place."

"And you're *you*—fierce, protective, so smart, sometimes you're stupid...with your heart in the right place."

"Not then." An admission. A difficult one to make given the fallout...and his son's death. Guilt rose bright and blinding. Grief and self-loathing lashed him like a long-tailed whip. "I fucked up, Theo."

"We all do, handsome. Can't go back, gotta go forward. Part of that is sharing the pain and maybe, finally, being able to forgive yourself," she said, relaxing him one caress at a time. "Newsflash, Sloan...you're not perfect. Neither am I. No one is. We all mess up. The thing you need to get is, you're no longer alone. We're in this together. Start acting like it."

"You like busting my balls?"

"Stop stalling."

"You like busting my balls," he muttered.

"If doing it gets you where you need to be, then, yeah, absolutely."

Slipping his hand under the fall of her dark hair, he cupped the nape of her neck. The other dipped beneath the hem of her t-shirt. He palmed her bottom, drew her closer, then stroked up until his palm rested against her lower back.

The Meridian ignited.

Tingles swept over his skin.

With a groan, he nestled in, pressing his mouth to her temple. The connection he shared with her solidified. The electrostatic bands hummed. Magic burned through his veins as the floodgates opened, inundating him with pleasure.

Hands skating over his skin, she murmured his name.

He shivered in response. Goddess, she was glorious. So beautiful in her acceptance, she overwhelmed him every time he touched her.

"I love you, Theo."

"I know, honey. I love you too."

Absorbing her steadiness, Sloan drew her scent into his lungs. "Ready?"

"Sock it to me."

A laugh escaped him. How? No clue.

He didn't feel like laughing, but somehow her flippant comment lightened the load, coaxing him out of the darkness. Surprising in some ways. Completely expected in others. His mate excelled at settling him in ways he never would've thought possible before meeting her.

Step by step, Theodora moved him toward

something better, until pitch black shifted to shades of gray, helping him navigate the devastation, making him realize she was right. It was time. His reckoning was long overdue. So instead of shying away, Sloan opened the door to his past, connecting with his mate in the way of his kind. Hiding nothing, he let the memory flow from him into her, sharing the night that had tormented him for over a decade.

∼

STANDING in the arms of the man she loved, Theodora shivered with longing. The dread arrived next, pushing calm out, dragging the sense of impending impact in. The doom-scape was real. Alive in the Hub, gathering in Sloan's energy field, the harbinger that preceded emotional fallout. A detonation as devastating as the nuclear one everyone on earth feared as people continued to hate and countries continued to fight.

So many things about Sloan came easy.

The grief he carried wasn't one of them.

But she'd asked for it. Begged him to let her all the way in. To trust her to be strong enough to take what he gave when he laid himself bare. His fear of vulnerability broke her heart. Someone had taught him to be that way. She'd been taught the same by her uncle. A man without conscience or honor. A man who relished hurting others almost as much as he enjoyed strong whiskey. A man so unlike Sloan, she wondered how her mate had survived inside the hideous distortion of self-imposed isolation for so long.

He kept a lot hidden. So much buried deep. Too much left unsaid, trying to protect himself from the truth.

But that was over now.

His wound needed lancing.

She'd taken her shot by asking Daimler to babysit Violet, then cornering Sloan in the Hub. But now, with his heart pounding and grip on her firming, nerves got the better of her. Was she being too pushy? Too aggressive? Not direct enough? Would saying the same thing a different way garner the results she wanted…and he needed?

Hard to know, but one thing for sure—now that she'd started, she couldn't back down. She wanted to do right by her mate, which meant following through. No matter how painful the process or the wreckage in the aftermath, she was committed to the crash.

She sensed the spiral coming. Could feel the tidal wave of grief as recall forced him to relive that night.

"Sloan?"

He made a sound in the back of his throat. Agonizing. Awful. So stark, she pressed closer, fisting her hands in the back of his t-shirt.

"I'm here," she whispered, holding him tight. "I'm not going anywhere. Take your time."

"He was so tiny, Theo. So vulnerable without me and…" His voice broke as memory took over. His body stayed with her, in her arms, warming her through, but his mind…*God.* His mind went somewhere else. "I wasn't there. I didn't protect him."

She murmured reassurances. Not enough. Barely anything. Feeling helpless as he traveled into a wasteland full of torment.

He swayed against her, anguish threatening to take his knees out.

Her arms tightened around him.

"I can't. I can't," Sloan rasped, clinging to her like a drowning man would a life raft. "There are no words. No right ones."

"Then don't use them. Show me instead."

"I don't want you to have that image in your head."

"I want to meet him," she said, holding the line, refusing to back down. "Let me meet your son, honey."

Another agonized sound.

A moment of hesitation, then...

He drew a deep breath and stopped resisting. Turning his face into her hair, he slid his hands beneath her shirt. His calloused palms whispered across her bare back. One went high. The other swept low, slipping beneath the hem of her lace underwear to cup her behind. Pleasure shivered through her, bringing relief but also telling a story so heartbreaking, the edges of perception darkened.

She closed her eyes and nestled closer, pressing her breasts to his chest and her head beneath his chin. Lips moving against his throat, she encouraged him to be brave. To let her help carry the load.

Taunt muscles flexed around her. He released a shaky breath, and she braced. The world fell away, leaving her suspended in space, narrowing until she knew nothing but him. The cold floor beneath her feet ceased to exist. The low hum in the computer lab disappeared. Now she floated, warm in his arms, safe in his sphere as he connected in ways only a Dragonkind warrior could.

The Meridian, the source that nourished all living things, flexed.

The pulse rippled across the gateway of her mind.

Warm current ran up her spine. Pleasure curled deep. Satisfaction rose hard. A second later, Sloan slipped inside her mind. He hovered a moment, allowing her adjust, then...

Mental tether hooks struck. He tugged, testing the connection. Breathtaking beauty trickled through, stealing her breathe. As the intensity rose, he turned a mental dial, upping the wattage, forging deeper, melding his consciousness with hers.

Instinct wanted her to fight the invasion. Experience stilled the need. She accepted what he offered with gratitude, drifting into a riptide of emotion, leaning into the power of energy-fuse, holding him steady, following where he led.

Energy-fuse. God. Incredible. Unlike anything she'd ever felt, but knew now, she couldn't live without. Terrifying in some ways. The most natural thing in the world in others. The bond she shared with Sloan was strong. Unbreakable. Present in all she did, but occupying the same cerebral space with him counted as something else. Something more. Something better.

She shivered as sensation tunneled, drawing her away from the here and now. She landed in another place and time. South Texas. Eleven years ago. In the heat and dust, inside a city she'd never visited yet felt familiar.

Tangled up with Sloan, she sank further into his flow, becoming him, abandoning herself as memory pushed images into her head. Tuned in, she watched the pictures flash on her mental screen. A black-haired beauty laughing. Light brown skin kissed by the wandering fingers of a full moon. Baby belly rounding out a tight t-shirt. Dark eyes sparkling up at her.

Amanda.

Her name was *Amanda*.

The moment the name entered her head, the image spun. Now, she was flying. Wings-spread wide. Scales rattling in unpredictable winds. Panic-stricken. Pushing the limits of speed and her strength as—

Thunder rumbled in the distance.

Exhaust fumes scored her senses as she rocketed out of a mountain pass. Thick clouds and fresh air gave way to smog. Cutting through the filth, she leveled out over a stretch of highway. Treetops thrashed above concrete sidewalks. Hot and heavy, wind ripped over her scales as she blasted across a night sky glowing bright with city lights. Narrow streets rolled into wider boulevards. Squat houses transitioned to apartment buildings, arrowing toward the office towers that stood around a park in the downtown corridor.

Focused on the sprawling complex in the distance, she banked into a tight turn and set up her approach. Nothing unusual about the place. The hospital was one of El Paso's finest, a tall building surrounded by a cluster of shorter ones. All interconnected, each serving a specific purpose, along with the humans who arrived for medical treatment at all hours of the day and night.

Cloaked by magic, invisible to human eyes, she flew over the main parking lot. Too many cars. Not the best place to land.

Contrails slicing off her wingtips, she circled back around. Her eyes narrowed on the tallest building. Lots of space to land on the rooftop. No need to make any adjustments in flight. Simply fly in, land hard, enter the complex, and find the floor that housed the maternity unit.

Battling a vicious updraft, Theodora folded her wings. Gravity yanked her out of the sky. Dry air whistled over her dark brown scales. Heat lightning struck, ripping through gathering clouds. Electricity sizzled above the city, making the horns on her head tingle as her paws slammed into the helipad. Steel groaned. The spikes riding her spine rattled. Asphalt tiles split, pushing sharp shards between her white talons.

Shaking the debris from her claws, she transformed, shifting from dragon to human form. With a murmur, she conjured her clothes. Jeans and a t-shirt settled on her skin as she stomped her feet into worn cowboy boots and jogged across the helipad. A quick jump down put her level with the rooftop entrance. Moving with purpose, she flicked her hand. Earth magic spilled from her fingertips. The glass doors slid open. Without breaking stride, she crossed the threshold and invaded the small lobby.

Two elevators to her left.

Five conjoined chairs to the right.

Heavy steel door standing sentry to the stairs straight ahead.

Gaze glowing bright green, she opened the door with her mind and entered the stairwell. Fast feet took her down. Dread swirled up, making her heart thump and her mind scream. The denial was foolish. Nothing but a pipedream. With her sonar up and running, she already sensed Amanda. The friend she'd made her lover was in the facility, six stories down, in the north-east corner of the hospital, but...

It was too soon.

Way too soon.

Amanda was only six months along. Barely out of her second trimester, nowhere near ready to be inside a hospital for anything other than weekly checkups.

Hope collided with reality. Maybe she was wrong. Maybe it was nothing. Just a blip in an otherwise healthy pregnancy, but dread sent her sideways anyway. Carrying a Dragonkind infant wasn't easy. Most human females never made it through, and still, she wanted to believe the magic she fed Amanda each day had done its job. Hadn't worn off as she hunted the rogue in mountain passes. Was still keeping her safe even though it had been hours since she'd last seen her.

And yet, fear rose, feeding her worst-case scenarios.

Theodora tried to not to panic. Inventing problems wasn't wise. Hurrying the hell up, talking to the doctors, discovering the issue, setting it to rights, would serve her better.

Feet moving double-time, she rounded the last landing and vaulted down the steps. The slam-bang of her boots ricocheted, echoing off cinderblock walls as she cranked the door open and stepped into the ER.

The sharp scent of floor cleaner mixed with antiseptic hit her.

A quick scan provided more details.

Chaos absolute. Injured humans were everywhere. Some slumped in chairs, others sat on the floor while more stood leaning against pale walls. Nurses in colorful scrubs manned three intake windows with counter-to-ceiling plexiglass, trying to keep up with the influx of would-be patients. Doctors in white lab coats came and went from curtained off bays. Paramedics rushed in and out, some with empty gurneys, others with people in various states of consciousness.

Pivoting to the right, she left the calamity and rechecked her sonar. Still in the same place. Amanda hadn't been moved yet.

Raised voices quieted as she jogged past "DO NOT ENTER" signs and entered the brainstem of the ER. She paused on the lip of the room and took stock. Wide open area in the center with desks and computers. Messy piles of file folders laid out on every available surface. Private rooms fronted by glass walls and sliding doors running along both sides of the room.

Thick in the air, the scent of Amanda's blood reached her.

With a curse, she followed the trail. Around a corner. Up another flight of stairs. Into a long corridor. Her boots thumped across industrial grade linoleum. Powerful magic did the rest, clearing a path in front of her. Doors opened, then closed on silent hinges. Cloaking spell still up and running, she wove her way between rushing doctors and nurses, hugging the walls to avoid trampling hospital staff.

The scent path grew stronger.

Her focus narrowed on a set of swinging doors at the end of the hall.

Stepping around a stack of the plastic wrapped, unpacked boxes, she bumped into an office chair. Wide seat. Tall back. Covered in purple leather. Kneeing the armrest, she set it spinning on roller wheels out of her way. Slamming into the wall, it whirled back in her direction. She shoved it again and pushed through the doors into an antechamber. Long stainless-steel sink in front of her with sharp smelling soap resting a ledge, a run of wide windows above it.

More doors to her right.

A high-tech operating suite beyond both.

Without breaking stride, she crossed the threshold. Her boot soles hit slick and slid on linoleum. Not understanding, she regained her balance and glanced down. Blood on the floor. Pools of it surrounding an operating table draped in blue sheets, surrounded by humans wearing surgical scrubs, masks and—

"Call it, Dr. Finnley."

The breath left her body. Her mind went blank.

A loud exhale. The snap of latex gloves. "Time of death…8:43pm."

"The baby?"

"No," someone inside the suite murmured, tone trailing sorrow. "He didn't make it."

"Goddamn it," the surgeon whispered. "How did we lose them both?"

"She bled out," a nurse said. "Catastrophic cardiac event."

"I know that, Sandy." His brow furrowed. The surgeon glared at his assistant over his mask. "But how?"

"No clotting factor," someone else said. "Nothing in her blood panel suggested any problems before she went into v-fib."

Feet rooted to the floor, she shook her head in denial. It couldn't be true. She didn't want it to be true, but then, the operating team's words registered. *Bled out. Unable to clot. Time of death. God…God…God.* The healing power of earth magic hadn't helped at all. None of her precautions mattered. Nothing she'd done to keep Amanda stable, to prevent her death had—

"Fuck," the surgeon muttered, snapping his gloves off. "I want an autopsy to confirm. Full investigation."

Silence met the pronouncement.

Machines defied the quiet, humming as the human rabble stood unmoving around Amanda.

No beep on the heart rate monitor. No breath in her lungs. The devastating smell of death hovering in the air. A nurse moved, breaking through the silent coven to set a swaddled bundle with a blue hat on the table next to her friend's body.

The horror held her suspended before...

Rage and shock ripped through it, tearing at the edges of her mind.

A rumble started inside her head, then grew and deepened as grief carved her open. Bleeding pain, she screamed. Trapped inside the cloaking spell, no one heard her, but magic spilled out, pouring from her veins into the room. The earth answered her anguish, striking like a poisonous sidewinder.

The hospital's foundation cracked.

The building shook.

The floor heaved.

Fissures opened seams in the walls. Metal tray tables flipped over. Surgical instruments went flying as high-powered lights swayed.

With a series of curses, the medical team abandoned their patient. Rubber soles leaving a bloody trail, humans streamed around her, exiting the OR as her knees hit the floor. Tears tightened the back of her throat. As each pooled in her eyes, she stared at her swaddled son laying lifeless on the table beside his dead mother.

God forgive her.

It was her fault. *All her fault.*

No matter how much Amanda wanted it, she should've stayed away. Held the line and said no. Instead, she'd caved under the pressure, giving her friend what she wanted, needing to be needed, and become delusional in the process. And as the building trembled and lights winked out, she tipped her head back and railed at the unfairness. At the brutal truth of what she'd done. She screamed until she grew hoarse and could no longer breathe.

A sob escaped her.

Swamped by grief and guilt, she crawled through blood to the edge of the table. Grasping the edge, she pulled herself up, tears spilling over as she cupped Amanda's cheek and picked up her son.

"I'm sorry," she rasped. "So fucking sorry."

But it was too late for regret.

Her friend lay dead. Their son hadn't lived.

Leaning in, she kissed Amanda softly, said goodbye, and cradling her son, stumbled from the room. Numb, unseeing, feet slipping on blood, she careened across the antechamber, out into the hallway. Spotting the purple chair, she sank into leather seat. Hunched over, she stared at his small face. Sheer perfection. Beauty that would never be realized.

Rocking him gently, she named him Simeon, and pain shearing her soul, started to sing. Slow. Soft. Each note full of love and longing. Giving her son his first and last lullaby.

THE SONG from that day played like a death knell inside his head. Melancholy in the melody. Sorrow in each chord. Devastation in the lyrics, giving voice to his pain, saying the things he found impossible to say.

There were no words.

No way to express the depth of his anguish.

Though, he knew the song by heart.

Rising and falling with the strum of acoustic guitar, Sloan hummed along. He felt the rasp in the back of his throat. Tasted the tears on his lips. Knew the weight of his son in his arms, still warm from his mother's womb, and relived the torment of loss.

Every day.

Always the same regret.

Forever the same result.

He carried it with him like a talisman. Holding the memory inside his heart instead of his head. Living it. Breathing it. Becoming it as he drifted through a world without his son. He kept him close in the waking hours. Saw Simeon's face in his dreams when he slept, knowing he should've been there. Instead, he'd arrived too late to save their lives.

The mother of his child was gone. So was his son. Buried twelve years ago beneath the hard, cold Texas ground. Had he been brave enough, he would've joined them. The drive to live had stopped him. The sense of something more did the rest, helping him hold on while he hunted for a purpose.

The night he met Bastian and the Nightfury dragon warriors proved his desperate belief in *something more* true. He'd been resurrected and reborn, been gifted brothers. Warriors he loved and valued. The pack had saved his life, shifting his focus, providing a target, giving him an outlet for his grief and aggressive nature.

Knowing it, though (being grateful for Bastian's intervention), didn't stop him from playing a game of *what if*, longing for a different outcome for his son. Incredibly long odds given human females rarely survived birthing Dragonkind.

His soul didn't care about facts. It followed a different beat, crying out, reaching back in time, wishing, wanting, desperate for the impossible. For Simeon to live. For him to know the pleasure of raising his child.

The lead singer reached the crescendo.

His heart ached harder.

His son had turned twelve yesterday.

He commemorated it the same way he always did—alone. Given his sins, he didn't deserve anything else. He knew Theodora wouldn't agree. She loved him too much to let him suffer alone. In the dark. Suffocating in the silence.

The entire reason he hadn't told her.

His mate looked after him, twisting herself in knots to give him what he needed. Night in. Night out. She kept him steady. During the days too, holding fast while he slept, smoothing out his nightmares, giving him sweeter dreams. A tremendous gift. One he thanked the goddess for all the time. She'd been made for him. He'd been born to ensure she thrived, so no matter how hard, he would—

"It's The Tragically Hip."

Her voice dragged him from the past, bridging time and space. Dragged out of the purple chair in the hospital corridor, he landed inside his body. His mind followed. The song stopped playing as he realized where he stood—inside Black Diamond's computer lab, her scent in his nose, his arms tight around her, with his palms pressed to the softest skin he'd ever touched.

Humming the tune against the base of his throat, she swayed in time. "Fiddler's Green. You sang him Fiddler's Green."

"Yeah."

"Beautiful."

His chest tightened at her words. He'd hoped…hoped so hard…that he'd done right. That the song he'd chosen for Simeon had done his son justice.

"A lullaby about a little boy taken too soon." Shifting in his arms, she pulled back enough to look up at him. Lashes wet with tears. Expression full of sorrow. Understanding shining in her green eyes. "Perfect choice, honey."

Slipping from beneath her shirt, he gathered her long hair in his hand and pulled it over her shoulder. Comforted by the softness, he twirled his fingers in the thick strands. "I didn't know what else to do."

A tear rolled, leaving a wet trail across his skin.

Theodora kissed it away, and staying close, held his gaze. "He was beautiful."

"I know."

"Do you want to go get him?"

His brows collided. "What?"

"Bring him and Amanda here," she said. "Have them closer. Be able to visit whenever you want."

Shock thumped through him. *Bring them here? To Seattle?* He opened his mouth. No sound came out. Unable to find his voice, Sloan stared at her.

"You've never considered it?"

Finding it hard to breathe, he shook his head.

"Why not?"

"I don't know. I just…"

As he trailed off, she tilted her head. A dangerous glint entered her eyes a moment before they narrowed on him. "A form of punishment? A way to make yourself suffer more?"

Hearing the edge in her tone, he swallowed. "Not exactly, but—"

"You don't deserve that, Sloan. You deserve to have your loved ones close."

He didn't agree.

He deserved that and much worse for what he allowed to happen. Faced with the rising tempest of her temper, though, wasn't the time to press his point. A smart decision. The second he told her he didn't deserve her compassion and understanding, she'd get pissy, insist it wasn't his fault, but…

It was.

All of it.

He'd been the cause of it all. Amanda's pain and suffering. His son's brutal death. Had he been more disciplined, less malleable, none of it would've happened.

His mate scowled. "I know what you're thinking, Sloan. And I'm telling you to stop it."

"Theo—"

"You didn't murder her. Or kill your son. Get that out of your head," she said, planting her hands flat on his chest to punctuate her point. "What happened was tragic. Awful. You did all you could for Amanda and Simeon."

"I never should've slept with her."

"Did you rape her?"

"No!" The denial exploded from his chest. "Never. I would never—"

"Did you lie to her?"

He shook his head. "She knew I was Dragonkind. I told her about energy-fuse and what it meant. She believed we'd forged that connection, and I was too young to know the difference. We were best friends. I loved her. I thought that would be enough, and the Meridian would prove that true at the realignment."

"I'm sorry," she whispered, tone full of tenderness.

Another round of pain hit him, making it difficult to breathe. "Me too."

"I need you to hear me, Sloan. Listen. Really take it in." Raising her hands, she cupped his face and drew him closer. Nose-to-nose with him, her gaze bore into his. "Free will, honey. Amanda wanted you. Even knowing the risks, she chose you. I don't blame her. All that is you...the beauty you bring...even without the bond we share, I would've risked it too."

His throat clogged. "Fuck, baby."

"I know it's heavy. I know you can't forget. I don't want you to deny the loss, and the grief you feel because of it. Amanda's a part of you, so honor her by accepting her choice and forgiving yourself for letting her make it. By doing that, you cherish the life you made together. And Simeon deserves that kind of reverence from his father."

"Shit."

"Yeah," she whispered. "Can't change it, handsome. Can't go back, gotta move forward. They're your family, Sloan. You need to bring them here where you can be close to them."

He drew a shaky breath. "No one knows. I haven't told the pack."

"Time to do that, then. You're gonna need their help bringing Simeon and Amanda home."

Another tear tipped over his bottom lashes.

She wiped it away. "All right?"

He nodded.

"Good." Approval in her eyes, she kissed him softly. Gently. With so much feeling, the heartache that always plagued him lessened. Not a lot. A tiny bit, but the relief gave him hope, along with place to start. "Now…you wanna go help our daughter pick raspberries?"

"She's awake?"

"Daimler's in the greenhouse with her."

One hand in her hair, the other still cupping her bare ass-cheek, he gave her a squeeze. "You going to put on pants?"

"Do you want me to?"

"No, I love your ass. Watching it's one of my favorite pastimes, but the pack's stirring," he murmured, sensing movement in the lair as his brothers rolled out of bed to start the day. "They'll appreciate you covering up since the instant any of them stare at your legs, I'll be force to retaliate."

"How?"

"By ripping their faces off."

She grinned. "I'll put on pants."

"Appreciated."

"Conjure me some?"

He smiled, enjoying the fact his mate loved when he used magic. Abilities that ranged from end-of-the-world destructive to charmingly innocuous. One of which included conjuring clothes out from thin air. Taking his hand out of her boy shorts, he murmured his wishes. Heat flowed like liquid fire through his veins. Calm settled deep, smoothing over jagged lines of grief as his mental vault opened. A pair of soft sweatpants the color of her eyes appeared in his hand.

She gasped in wonder.

His smile turned into a grin as he stepped back and handed them to her. Delight in her eyes, she accepted the dark green joggers, then hopped into the pair one leg at a time while he enjoyed the show.

With a sharp tug, she tied the drawstring. "All good. I like this brand. They're super soft."

"Good," he said, watching her adjust the waistband. "Ready to go find Vivi?"

"In a minute." Finished tucking the string under, she glanced up. Her gaze collided with his, making him brace. "One last thing."

He raised a brow in question.

"I don't care how ugly it is, your chair stays.

You held Simeon for the first and last time in it. Sang him a lullaby in it. We're never letting it go."

Sloan closed his eyes. Fucking hell. His mate. She was beyond beautiful. Exactly what he needed, all he'd ever wanted, a gift he didn't deserve.

Theodora understood without him having to explain. The chair he sat in every day was his only connection to the past. To his son and the female who loved him so much, she gave her life to give Sloan a family. And even though Theodora was right—Amanda had made her own choices, gone in with her eyes wide open—he still should've known better.

But then, hindsight was twenty-twenty.

He couldn't have known then what he knew now, and as Theodora took his hand and led him out of the Hub, Sloan knew he must to find a way to forgive himself. Otherwise, he'd remain mired in the past, unable to move forward, diminishing the memory of Amanda and his son. He needed to honor them in the way of his kind. Both deserved to be here, with him at Black Diamond. To be known by the warriors he called brothers. Males who loved him, and he loved in return. Hiding his past dimmed their importance to him, making a mockery of the family he found when he joined the Nightfury pack.

It had taken time, but now, Theodora's message came through loud and clear.

Burdens weren't meant to be carried alone.

Lacing his fingers with hers, Sloan tugged her closer and dipped his head. His mouth touched down on the top of her head. "Thank you for setting me straight."

"Anytime, honey." Wrapping her free hand around his biceps, she pressed her forehead into the side of his shoulder. "I have your back. Always and forever."

Always and forever.

Sounded exactly right.

"I love you, Theodora."

"I love you too, Sloan."

And just like that, the last of his sorrow washed away. It would come again. It always did, but as his world tilted upright on its axis, he embraced the truth. Nothing was ever perfect, but with Theodora in his life, he could cope. Could hold out hope. One day the grief would lessen. One day the good memories he and Amanda made before it went wrong would resurface. One day, he'd forgive himself for the loss of his son. Until then, he had a daughter to spoil and raspberries to pick.

Read more of Sloan and Theodora's story in FURY OF AGGRESSION.

Buy your copy today!

500 MILES

A DRAGONFURY SHORT STORY

1

MONTEREY, CALIFORNIA—IN A SMALL HOUSE BY THE BAY

He'd told her to stay away.

Said it flat out. Tone firm. Gaze steady. Expression set. The warning clear in the line of his body as he made her promise to run far. To run fast. And never return.

His rejection had been a tough pill to swallow.

She hadn't wanted to leave then. But this was now. And given the seriousness of her situation, Natalie Kristiansen knew doing what he asked wasn't feasible anymore. The longer she stayed away, the worse things got. Which meant she needed to be brave and follow her heart. One more time. No matter how much his reaction to her return cost her in the end.

Picking up the duffle bag at her feet, she glanced toward the bank of windows. Tall panels. Framed in black. An uninterrupted stretch of glass that showcased a world class view.

She paused to enjoy it for the last time. West coast currents churned under sunlit water. Rolling waves curled into whitecaps, frothing at the tips near the shoreline. An ache tightened her chest. The ocean understood up and downs, all the peaks and valleys life threw at a person. As she watched the rise and fall, it seemed to her, dark waters mirrored her heartache. Every bit of pain and uncertainty. All her worries as she stood still and silent, struggling to understand the depths of it herself.

Clutching the house keys in her hand, she dragged her gaze from the Pacific and turned to leave. The quick pivot made her dizzy. Nausea kicked up, throwing bile into the back of her throat. A horrible taste surfed into her mouth. She stopped, fighting the need to throw up, and reached out to steady herself.

Keys jangled as her hand landed on the kitchen island. Cooled by the hum of a powerful air conditioner, the quartz countertop slid across her palm. The solid surface helped her breathe through the upheaval. Inhale through her nose. Exhale out her mouth. Wait for the spinning to stop. A circuit she navigated daily in recent weeks.

The topsy-turvy settled.

Her equilibrium returned.

Relieved by the quick rebound, she left the keys where they landed for her landlord, swung the bag over her shoulder, and moved down the narrow corridor to the front door. A quiet click, a sharp tug, and the weathered wooden panel swung wide, releasing her into open air.

The smell of saltwater hit her first.

Warm afternoon sun stroked over her next, chasing away the chill, as she stopped on the landing and looked out over the gravel drive. Toward her truck. Toward escape. Toward what she hoped would be the rest of a very long life.

Something that was never guaranteed.

Something she believed Hamersveld had the power to make happen.

Breaking her word to him didn't come easy. She understood the danger—the threat her reappearance in his life represented—but refused to turn away. Dire circumstances dictated the path. She needed him now. Was in the worse sort of trouble. The kind instinct warned she wouldn't survive without him by her side. Staying away, living her life without him in a small house overlooking the Bay of Monterey, was no longer an option. The only one available to her now involved finding and convincing him before she ran out of time.

A death-grip on the railing, she adjusted the duffle bag strap on her shoulder, and feet tapping on wooden treads, made her way down a steep set of stairs. Carefully. Slowly. Terrified of taking a tumble and splitting her skull open on the flagstone path below. A distinct possibility given her shaky state. To be expected, she guessed, given she carried—

Her phone rang.

Halfway across the driveway, she tugged the iPhone from her back pocket. Flipping it upright, she glanced at the locked screen. Dread rose hard. Her stomach clenched as she went nine rounds with unease, flipping through a deck called *Worse Case Scenarios*. She debated a moment. Ignore the call? Let it go to voicemail or answer it?

The ringtone trilled again.

Blowing out a long breath, she settled her emotions and tapped go.

"Hello?"

"Natalie?"

"Hey, Doc."

"Ah, hey," Dr. Angles said, a note of hesitancy in the voice. OB-GYN to the rich and famous, the doctor had a reputation around town. She was the best of the best. Competent. Professional. Personable while bringing excellence to her work. Natalie liked Dr. Angles the instant she met her. "Just checking in to see how you're feeling."

"Pretty crappy."

"I need you to come in."

Natalie frowned. "To the clinic?"

"Community Hospital off Highway 68. I want to run more tests."

"Why?" Stupid question given she'd had blood work done two days ago. Her levels must be off. Irregular. Off baseline. Or something. Made sense given the way she felt—and what intuition kept telling her. "How bad is it?"

Silence came over the line, then...

"I'd like you to come in. How soon can you get here?"

All right, then. No need to sugarcoat it.

Whatever was in her bloodwork landed north of bad. *Really, really bad.* Which meant she didn't have time to spend in a hospital. Human medicine wouldn't help. As good as she was, Dr. Angles, and her tests, wouldn't save her. She needed Hamersveld—his touch, his time, his bio-energy—

to sustain her through the coming months. To stop her slow slide into a nasty decline. She'd delayed long enough, wanting to be sure before she broke her promise, rolled back into Seattle, and disrupted his life.

"Natalie?"

"Give me an hour," she said, lying through her teeth to get off the line and on the road. "Where am I meeting you?"

"The ER. Give the nurse at reception your name. She'll bring you to me right away."

"Okay."

"And Natalie?"

"Yeah?"

"Don't worry. I've got you covered. Everything's going to be all right."

"Thanks, Dr. Angles."

"See you in a bit."

Bleeping the locks on her F-150, Natalie popped the door open and swung inside. What she didn't do was answer. She'd already lied to Dr. Angles once. No need to compound the issue and do it again. So instead, she signed off by saying a heartfelt "goodbye", then fired up her truck and pointed it north. Toward Seattle. Toward the man-dragon who'd wanted her once, but might not anymore. Weeks had passed without contact. Doubt had crept in, eroding her confidence, making her question every moment she spent with him.

Would he be happy to see her again? Or annoyed?

Would he want their child? Or ask her to—

Natalie shook her head to shake the horrible

thought loose. No. No way. She refused to entertain the possibility. A smart decision given she couldn't go back and change it. Didn't want to either, so…

Onward.

Into the fray.

Barreling straight into the jaws of uncertainty. Hearing the miles fall away beneath the hum of oversized tires. Closing the distance between her and Hamersveld, regardless of the fact he'd warned her to never come back.

2

28 WALTON STREET—LATE AFTERNOON,
THE RAZORBACK LAIR

Five stories below ground, tucked away from deadly UV rays, Hamersveld exited his bedroom and turned into the main corridor. A highway of sorts, one that funneled his packmates toward the heart of the Razorback home —the kitchen where he and his packmates ate together each afternoon.

Boots thumping over limestone tiles, he kept his pace steady, using the walk to modulate his mood, but...

No joy in the journey. An abysmal attempt at self-regulation.

Lack of sleep didn't help. Neither did his nature. The constant need to kill someone never took a break, keeping violent tendencies close to his surface. An asset during the night while out hunting. Not so great in recent weeks with the Nightfury pack lying low and no targets in the sky.

Enter Denzeil.

The crafty little prick was an excellent place to paint a bull's-eye. The safest way for him to vent…and had been for weeks with good reason. The male had earned his attention by sticking his nose where it didn't belong. But as Hamersveld strode up the hall, it became apparent disappointment hovered on the horizon. He sent out an exploratory ping anyway, hoping he was wrong. Magic rippled out in concentric circles, washing over everything it touched and—

He scowled.

His dragon half had called it.

Denzeil wasn't inside the lair. The coward had flown the coop before dawn, desperate to avoid being trapped inside the city lair with Hamersveld. Not a bad move. Smart given he was grounded by daylight, unable to move until night pushed the sun out of the sky.

An annoying twist of circumstance he accepted.

All Dragonkind warriors did.

Prolonged exposure to UV rays was dangerous. Sunlight equaled blindness, followed by an agonizing death for his kind. Which made traveling by night a necessity, so…yeah. Denzeil might be an idiot, but he wasn't stupid, denying him what he needed most right now—a ball-busting fight in which he broke more of the whelp's bones.

A shame.

Frustrating too as he turned a corner. The space opened up. Cloud white walls arched into fifteen-foot ceilings. Recessed lighting led the way, drawing him past unoccupied bedrooms closed in by solid wooden doors, then past the entrance into Ivar's laboratory. Magic rumbling in his veins, he scanned the space without entering. No heat signature. No lethal vibe. His best friend, commander of the Razorback pack, wasn't playing mad scientist today.

Eyes narrowed, he deepened the search and—

Not inside the lair, either.

His friend must be across the street, inside the little A-frame, availing himself of Sasha Cooper's charms…along with the softness of her bed.

"Good for him," he muttered as an ache opened behind his breastbone.

Looked like jealousy.

Smelled like jealousy.

It wasn't.

Envy played a part, sure. So did grief. Neither kept him from being happy for his friend. Ivar deserved a female to call his own. Someone who helped him take the edge off. Someone who encouraged him to relax. And if his friend found contentment in the arms of a blonde dynamo obsessed with the environment and saving bats, all the better.

The pang in his gut wasn't about that—or anyone else. It came from a deep inside him, welling up each time he acknowledged what he'd lost. Ivar's love affair shone a spotlight on the truth, making regret rise and pain spiral. He'd been suffering for weeks, fighting despair, denying the heartbreak, struggling to get back to baseline.

Nothing worked except fighting. Expressing the anguish physically expelled the excess energy. He needed the break along with the distraction. Denzeil's transgression served that role, providing an outlet, allowing him to direct his wrath at a guilty party.

He growled.

The yellow-bellied prick. If the male had any balls at all, he would've stood strong. Taken his licks. Instead, the Razorback IT expert skirted responsibility for his actions by hiding behind Ivar, citing pack protocol. Regulations that stated Hamersveld as Ivar's number two couldn't beat the snot of the warriors under his command.

Pansy-ass rule.

One he'd spent the last two months ignoring.

Reaching the end of the hallway, he turned left. The smell of roast beef and garlic bread hit him. His stomach growled as he stalked beneath the high arch into the kitchen. Three sets of eyes swung in his direction.

His gaze narrowed on the trio. "Where'd he go?"

The bravest of the three, Rampart raised a dark brow. "Who?"

"Don't fuck around, Ram." He curled his hands into fists. His knuckles cracked. The sharp snap-snap-snap echoed like warning shots as he eyeballed his friend. "Unless you want me to switch focus."

His packmate's mouth curved. "Could use the exercise."

The casual comment took the wind out of his sails. Hamersveld frowned. Was the male yanking his chain? Actually *teasing* him, a lone dragon with a reputation so bad Dragonkind warriors all kitchen island. "As far away from you as possible, I imagine."

"Good plan, given the looks of you." Ass-planted on one of the low-back stools, oversized mug in hand, Midion sipped his coffee. Black gaze locked on him, he hummed as brew strong enough to blow a lesser male's hair back, hit his taste buds. "You need to calm the fuck down, Sveld. Have a drink. Get laid. Something. *Anything* as long as it improves your mood."

Get laid.

Hristos, if only it were that simple. Too bad an easy fix wasn't a possibility for him. Only one thing would elevate what ailed him, and he'd sent her away.

"Beating the shit out of D isn't the answer, brother. Neither is hunting Nightfuries...or releasing some pressure by fighting with me," Rampart murmured, talking sense, making him want to hammer the male so hard his teeth hit the floor. "You need to find her. To soothe your dragon half by wrapping yourself up in her. Nothing else is going to work."

The words hit him center mass. A pain-filled sound escaped him.

On high alert, Midion took another sip. "Any idea where she went?"

Breathing through the anguish, Hamersveld shook his head.

"What about an alias?" Syndor asked. "You got a name we can chase?"

Against his will, the name streamed into his head.

over the world refused to approach, never ╷
tangle with him.

Not that he blamed them.

His past wasn't pretty. Uncaring who he ╷
he'd left death and destruction in his wake
decades. Pain, after all, bred more of the s
Years spent without friends. No pack to cal
own. Zero kinship or the chance for camaradei

Simple things.

Necessary things.

Things now that he had them, Hamers
didn't want to live without. An unexpected re‹
tion. He'd moved through the world alone for
turies, existing without really living, until he
Ivar and joined the Razorback pack. So, the
Rampart felt comfortable enough to razz him i
current mood counted as progress. Surprising
also welcome. The male's comfort level told
clearer than anything else he was accepted anc
preciated, trusted despite his brutal nature.

"Nightfall. You and me, Sveld," Rampart
anticipation in his eyes. "Two, maybe three ro›
of dragon combat training."

"You're on. Don't say I didn't warn you."

Rampart smiled.

He scowled and strode farther into the kitc
"But that doesn't answer my original questic
where did Denzeil go? The lair in the Cascades

Unfazed by his hard tone, Rampart shrugge

He bared sharp canines in warning.

Reacting to the show of aggression, Sy›
sidestepped, taking cover behind the long lengt

Natalie Kristiansen.

Love of his life. The lifeblood running through his veins. His first, last and only from now on. His everything. The entire reason he shied away from hunting her down. He'd given her his word. Risked his life and position inside the Razorback pack to ensure she stayed safe. No matter how much it hurt...or how much he missed her...he refused to break his promise. Natalie deserved to live a good life far from the dangers of Dragonkind.

Natalie.

Kristiansen.

Gorgeous name. As beautiful as the female who now possessed it.

Her first name was human given, written on her original birth certificate. The surname, however...

He swallowed past the lump in his throat.

Her last name was special. One that had belonged to his mother, and he'd gifted Natalie when he set up her new identity. So yeah, he knew the name she'd adopted before he forced her to flee Seattle.

Leaning against the kitchen island, Rampart frowned. "Sveld—"

"I can't."

"What you can't do is go on like this." Understanding in his pale blue eyes, Rampart met his gaze. "You refuse to feed. You hardly sleep. You're fixated on her. In need. In pain. So short tempered the warriors Ivar's given you to combat train walk on eggshells whenever you're around."

"With good reason," Syndor muttered. "No one's stupid enough to mess with a—"

"Surly water dragon," Midion said, finishing his packmate's sentence. "Scale-splitting nasty. Fun to watch in action, though."

Ignoring the byplay, Rampart stared at him, refusing to back down. "Ivar doesn't want to have this conversation with you. He loves you. Doesn't know how to talk about it without hurting you, so—"

"Ram," he growled.

"It falls to me," Rampart said, sailing past the interruption. "I'm your friend. Your brother-in-arms. We're new to it, but I care about you. I hate the path you're on, man. You're going to end up dead if you don't figure out how to rein it in."

With a sigh, Hamersveld bowed his head, knowing Rampart was right. He wasn't handling the loss of Natalie well. He ached for her, so much some nights he wished for death, desperate to stop the pain. And yet, he struggled to talk about it. To invite the males he trusted into his head—into his heart—for fear of being perceived as weak. Now, though, the door was open. Which left him with a choice—accept the help he needed and be honest. Or continue to be reckless and die alone in open skies when the Nightfuries attacked.

He sat with the idea for a moment, then put his feet in gear. His footfalls echoed, bouncing off dark cabinetry. His heart thumped, hammering the inside of his chest as unease cascaded through him. Quieting the urge to turn away, he joined his packmates at the island. Shoving two stools out of his way, he folded forward and leaned in. His forearms touched down on polished granite. A chill skated over his skin. Courage surfaced, warming him, dragging a decision up from the depths of his soul.

Chest so tight it hurt to breathe, he whispered, "I don't want to hurt her."

Rampart frowned. "I know, but—"

"If I hunt her down and bring her back, I take her life. Natalie dies here," he said, needing to make the warriors he fought beside every night understand. "I'd rather live my life knowing she's out there somewhere—happy, healthy and whole—instead of dead."

"Who says she's happy?" Rampart asked, challenging his assumption. "Maybe she misses you... needs you...is suffering without you as much as you are without her."

Syndor grunted in agreement.

"Fucking A," Midion muttered, swirling the dredges of coffee at the bottom of his mug. "Strong bond, powerful reaction. The way you're reacting means she accepted you. Probably had just as strong a reaction to you as you did to her."

Throwing him a sidelong look, Syndor asked, "Is Midion wrong?"

"No," he murmured, feeling the truth of it in his gut.

"She might be in pain, brother." Blue eyes boring into his, Rampart turned to face him. Mirroring his position, he leaned in, planting his elbows on the counter. "Can you live with that? Can you honestly say she's better off without you?

That having Natalie in your life isn't worth the risk?"

Worth the risk?

Hamersveld's brows collided. Could he live with the idea Natalie suffered without him? The question came. The pain went as his heart, mind and soul answered with a resounding NO.

His reaction, along with the instinct behind it, was selfish. Unhinged. Unconscionable, given the consequences. The second he claimed her in the way of his kind, she became a target. Being with him might well shorten her life. Then again, it might not.

He'd seen the mating mark on the Nightfury warriors in battle. Bastian and his band of bastards had cracked the code. His enemy possessed the answer to the ancient riddle of energy-fuse. The bond allowed a Dragonkind male to mate a female without hurting her, gifting him the ability to feed her the healing energy she needed to not only thrive during pregnancy, but also survive birthing a Dragonkind infant.

Vital information.

Essential to a warrior who loved his chosen female.

A possibility for him and Natalie if he uncovered the Nightfury pack's secret. Staring at the countertop, the beginnings of a plan surfaced. He needed to discover Bastian's weakness and force a confrontation. Capturing a member of Bastian's pack would force the Nightfury commander's hand. In exchange for the safe return of his warrior, Bastian would divulge the ins and outs of energy-fuse, providing what he needed to keep Natalie safe.

A good plan.

Not a great one considering Nightfuries continued to be scarce in the sky, but workable as long as Ivar agreed, he remained patient and—

Powerful energy sizzled across his senses.

His sonar went haywire.

Agony slashed at him.

With a curse, Hamersveld jerked upright. His dragon half snarled. The signal expanded, throbbing inside his skull, throwing him off balance. He stumbled sideways. The air heated. Magic blasted outward. Stools skittered on wooden legs. Battling the surge, he planted his feet, fighting to get his bearings as his brothers-in-arms surrounded him.

"What—"

"The—"

"Fuck, Sveld?"

The question didn't register. Voices ceased to matter as his sonar pinged again. He latched on. The fuzzy blip solidified inside his skull. His breath caught. His heart turned over. Thank the goddess. Natalie. She'd broken through the five-hundred-mile marker. Was close and getting closer. Each ping brought her further north, firmly inside his hunting circle, feeding him her location, allowing him to hook into the bio-energy she trailed like a long-tailed comet.

The signal screamed across his mental screen.

His dragon half roared in triumph.

Overwhelmed by the brutal onslaught, Hamersveld groaned and doubled over. Hands planted on his knees, he stared at the tops of his boots. "Hristos."

"What?" Midion said, half-bite, mostly bark. "What is it?"

Hitting his haunches beside him, Rampart leaned down to look him. "Talk, Sveld."

"Natalie," he rasped, struggling to breathe.

"What about her?" Setting up shop on his other side, Syndor palmed his shoulder.

"She..." he trailed off as the jagged signal smoothed out. The painful throb downgraded, unlocking his lungs. He drew a breath, then another as gratitude struck, pushing tears into his eyes. "She's close. On her way home."

"The five-hundred-mile marker?"

He nodded. "She just blew through it."

"An hour 'til nightfall," Midion said. "Think you can hold out 'til then or—"

"Do we need to lock you down?" Rampart asked, dread in his tone.

Clinging to the beauty of Natalie's signal, he shook his head, then fell forward. His knees hit the floor. His packmates cursed. Hands grabbed at him, holding him steady. He didn't care. Barely noticed the help. Breathing like a wounded animal, he rolled onto his back, going belly up in front of his brothers.

"Sveld?"

"Inform Ivar," he said, voice soft, order firm. "Wake the pack. The second night falls, we fly out as a unit."

The Razorbacks surrounded him grunted in agreement.

He barely heard them. Didn't care about their concern, or his prone position. He paid the vulnerability no mind. Only one thing mattered—the glorious burn of his female inside his head. So instead of moving, he stayed where he lay, palms up, legs spread, back pressed to the floor. Eyes closed, he listened to his packmates shuffle around him and clung to Natalie's signal. Hunting her energy. Tracking her movement. Following his female's progress as she broke her word, drove up I-5 and returned to him.

3

SOUTH TACOMA—THE DEAD-END OF
EASTER STREET

S tanding in a war room designed to take males apart, Zidane allowed the silence to settle on his skin. Across his senses. Closing his eyes, he soaked in the stillness, absorbing the soothing wave of a lair gone quiet.

A tingle ghosted down his spine. Flames followed, flickering over his shoulders, then down his bare back. Heat engulfed him. His dragon half sighed and sank deeper, relaxing as he opened his eyes and turned to his new knives. Seventeen strong, encased for the moment in hand-tooled leather sheaths, the assortment of blades came in all shapes and sizes. Some cleaver sized. Others as small as scalpels.

Works of art. The tools of his trade. The last pieces in the puzzle since his move across the Atlantic. Though the collection sat next to other toys, too. Straight and hooked pliers, narrow and wide chisels, different sized bone saws and wooden blocks. All set at precise intervals on the wooden tabletop he'd spent the last couple of weeks crafting.

A much nicer set-up than the one he left behind in Prague.

Thank the goddess. He'd always hated the dank despair of the dungeon room buried deep inside his sire's pavilion. Much preferred what he'd created here—a clean, aboveground space inside a windowless room that looked more like an operating suite than a torture chamber. Lovely lines. High ceilings. Easier to reach from his bedroom two floors up. Less electrical wiring to run too, which…he frowned…come to think of it, still needed to be done.

He'd already laid the cable. All he needed to do now was install the electrical plug that would connect the man-sized grill bolted to the only wall in the room comprised of concrete. A handmade piece, the apparatus stood ten feet tall and seven feet wide. Metal handcuffs already hung from top and bottom horizontal slats, waiting for the first visitor to be shackled in and strung up.

Anticipation shivered through him.

Impatience followed, urging him to fly out and begin the hunt.

Inhaling through his nose, he filled his lungs, enjoying the smell of new plaster and paint, then breathed out through his mouth. The need to make someone bleed downgraded from urgent to a pleasure-in-waiting. He needed to be smart. Do the research. Take his time. Ensure he won in the end by doing the heavy lifting upfront. Other males considered patience a virtue for a reason. And with renovations of the ramshackle mansion he shared with his packmates almost complete, he could afford the luxury…along with the delay.

Bastian and the Nightfury warriors weren't going anywhere.

Neither were Ivar and his motley crew of inept fighters.

Some way, somehow, he'd cull one of the bastards from the larger pack. The second he did, the enemy warrior would find himself inside his war room. Nothing but a plaything in a place designed to separate flesh from bone. No mercy shown. Zero breaks given.

Enlivened by the possibilities, he liberated a knife from its sheath. The handle settled in his palm like an old friend. He hummed. Perfect weight. Perfect length. Perfect weapon with which to—

A clang sounded.

Hinges creaked behind him.

The heavy steel door swung open.

Cradling the blade, fighting his need to throw it, Zidane glanced over his shoulder.

Blue eyes with yellow flecks narrowed on him. "You throw it at me, I gut you with it."

His mouth curved. "Tempting to put that to the test."

"Try me," Yakapov growled. "I'm begging you —*try me*."

Pivoting to face his first-in-command, he planted his ass on the table edge. With a flick, he tossed the knife. He watched it rotate above him. On revolution number three, he snagged it out of the air. Satisfaction struck, pushing bliss through his veins. A state of being Yakapov didn't share given the sour look on his face.

"Always so grumpy. What's wrong now, *zi kamir*?" he asked, calling his best friend "brother" in Dragonese. "Was the female not to your liking today? Not accommodating enough?"

"No stamina." Reliving the event, Yakapov scowled. "She didn't last through round two. I had to send her home in a cab."

"You mind-scrub her first?"

"Da," he said, thick Russian accent rolling. "Always. We don't want the females Montgomery finds to service us knowing where we sleep, but that's not the point."

He raised a brow. "What's the point?"

"I need more exercise. Fucking all day's fun, but it's getting old. I need blood on my claws."

"I'm working on it."

"The Razorbacks give up anything else?"

"The warriors Ivar loaned us don't know much. Three of the four are clueless, but one thing for sure..." Spinning the blade, he flipped it again. The perfect blend of craftmanship and beauty, the razor-sharp tip stayed upright, balanced on the pad of his index finger. "Blakmor knows more than he's saying."

"You going to take another shot at him?"

"Maybe," he said, then shrugged. "Though going toe-to-toe with him again might be a mistake."

Invading the Blakmor's mind had proven fruitful once, allowing him to steal the direct mind-speak link Ivar used to communicate with his pack. The connection allowed him to cherry-pick Razorback messages out of thin air every time Ivar started a new conversation. Very useful. A definite advantage. One he didn't want Ivar to know about, which meant being patient. He refused to play his hand too soon.

"Blakmor's smart, Yakapov. He's got a mind like a steel trap." Frowning, Zidane tilted his hand. The knife hilt collapsed against his palm. "His memory is coming back. I think he suspects he got more than just a blow job from the server at The Lucky Dog. If he figures out that I stole the Razorback link from him, he'll run to Ivar. The risk of what I might find during a second go at him isn't worth the reward."

His friend grunted in agreement.

"For now, we stay on track," he murmured. "Continue to build the shipping business. Sell the guns. Distribute the drugs. Acquire the wealth necessary to avoid the long reach of my sire."

"Rodin." The corner of Yakapov's lip curled, exposing a sharp canine. "Can't stand the meddling asshole."

Zidane huffed.

He understood his friend's reaction. Experienced a similar one whenever he spoke to his sire. Rodin, after all, was a taste most males never acquired.

As leader of the Archguard, his sire wielded a tremendous amount of power. The kind that spanned oceans and reached across continents. Nowhere was out of reach. No Dragonkind male was immune. If Rodin spoke, warriors listened or suffered the consequences...usually at Zidane's hand. But no longer. No fucking more. He'd put distance between himself and his sire. No way would he ever go back.

Agreeing to hunt Bastian after the high counsel labeled him a traitor by reinstating *Xzinile* (the ancient practice of exile, and the inevitable death of the warrior who refused to comply with an Archguard decree) had gotten him out of Prague to America.

An opportunity Zidane refused to squander.

After he killed Bastian and his merry band of bastards, he planned to stay. To eliminate the competition and clear the skies. The warriors he handpicked in Prague to follow him across the pond were part of the plan. A powerful group of males. Fierce. Smart. Loyal. Each possessed the kind of nasty streak he not only admired, but needed to succeed. The foundational pieces of a dragon pack he'd build into a dominate force on the West Coast of America. Not just among Dragonkind, but in human circles as well.

Rodin wouldn't be happy.

Zidane didn't care.

He had ambition and drive. And honestly, it was time. Time to actualize. Time to optimize. Time to embrace his destiny and fly free without his sire's constant interference.

Raking the hair out of his face, Yakapov retied the blond strands into a man-bun at the back of his head. "One other thing."

"Yeah?" Gaze on his friend, Zidane returned the knife to its sheath.

"The boys've been talking..." his friend hesitated, then said, "we need a name."

His brows collided. "A what?"

"A pack name. Something other than *Rodin's Death Squad*." Holding his gaze, Yakapov crossed his arms over his chest. "Bastian labeled his crew Nightfury. Ivar's got the Razorbacks. We need to define our pack in the same way, Zidane. With a new handle—one that tells outsiders exactly who we are."

The suggestion struck him as odd.

He opened his mouth, then closed it again.

No sense shutting down the idea without thinking about it first. He refused to fall into old patterns. The habit of pleasing his sire—of leaning away from self-sovereignty—was self-defeating. Unworthy of a commander. Though, the long-instilled programming was difficult to override.

Rodin was clever...and deliberate in his coercion. He'd spent years obliterating any sense of individuality. In Zidane. In the warrior packs living close to Prague. In the upper ranks of the Archguard, too. As leader, his sire ruled with a clenched fist and an iron will. In that world, what Rodin wanted not only trumped community needs but also those of the individual.

But that was over now.

Fate had dealt him a good turn by landing him in Tacoma. By giving him a new start, so...

What Rodin wanted for him and his squad no longer mattered. Despite the orders coming from the Archguard in Prague, Zidane possessed the power to choose.

Heart beating hard, he stared at his friend.

A pack name.

The first building block that would help him form an identity. A platform he could stand on while he seized control of his life, differentiating himself from Rodin and the high counsel. By naming his pack, he sent a clear message, making it plain he couldn't be manipulated...or forced to play Rodin's games—unless, of course, he chose to enter the arena.

Excitement skittered through him. Zidane tipped his chin. "Any suggestions?"

"A number," Yakapov said, looking as though he wanted to kill someone. "They're all shit."

"What about..." he paused. A plethora of possibilities tumbled through his mind. He settled on his favorite. "Emberclaw. Or maybe...Stormfire. We could add Dominion or Legion to the back end."

"Emberclaw Dominion. Stormfire Legion." Pursing his lips, Yakapov tilted his head. "Not bad."

"We'll bring it to a vote." Pushing out his lean against the table, he nodded. "See what the others think, then—"

Static attacked his temples.

Zidane jerked upright. His boot soles rasped across concrete as the hiss intensified. Pain tore his senses open. His dragon half responded, rearing inside him, slamming against the limits of its mental cage. Hanging on by a thread, Zidane shut his beast down and turned inward to track the signal.

Jagged spikes smoothed into a steady blip.

A link into mind-speak opened.

Rapid-fire chatter came through the line.

A single voice cut through the chaos. As the clarifying force expanded inside his head, Yakapov left his position by the door. The heavy thud of boots came at him. A hand clamped down on his shoulder. Grounded by his friend's grip, Zidane listened hard, concentrating on the orders being communicated through the link.

"What?" With a growl, Yakapov shook him. "What is it?"

"Ivar."

"He on the move?"

"Something's happening south of Portland."

"Oregon?"

He nodded, so focused on the signal his vision wavered. He lost sight of Yakapov in the blur, staring at his friend without actually *seeing* him. "The entire Razorback pack is flying out."

"Nightfuries in the mix?"

"Unknown."

"Sun's down. Sky's clear," Yakapov said. "We going?"

Dragon half frothing, Zidane refocused on his first-in-command. Bright blue eyes full of hope collided with his. He bared his teeth as aggression cratered his control. Magic slipped his net. Fire broke through the surface of his skin. Zidane welcomed the burn, loving the feel as flames raged down his spine. Heat blasted across the war room.

His eyes sparked, bathing Yakapov and the white walls in citrine glow.

Yakapov released him before fire scorched his hand.

With a snarl, Zidane pivoted toward the exit.

"Fantastic," his friend muttered, reading the intent driving his actions. "About time. Can't wait to sink my claws into someone."

The scent of smoke trailing behind him, Zidane cranked the door wide and crossed the threshold. He turned right into the main-floor hallway. His destination—the kitchen to gather his pack, then the back porch. No time to waste. He needed to shift into dragon form and get airborne as fast as possible.

The Razorbacks were already in full flight. Storming south. Crossing through territory he and his pack claimed, in search of someone driving up I-5.

He needed to know who.

He wanted to know why. Only then would he know who to kill and how many prisoners to take.

4

A death grip on the steering wheel, Natalie battled another round of nausea. Breathing in through her nose, she exhaled through her mouth. Mind over matter. Strength in the face of overwhelming odds. The approach should work. It usually did. But now, while driving mountain roads, the mental redirection didn't help. Each time the two-lane highway dipped, so did her stomach.

Swallowing the nasty taste, she continued deep-breathing, determined to stay on track. To stick to her timeframe and reach Seattle before dawn, but…

Bile touched the back of her throat.

She fought the urge to gag and—

"Damn it," she whispered, knowing she was almost out of time.

She needed to stop. Take a break and get out of the truck if she hoped to keep her latest meal down. The baby needed it. So did she if the world turned cruel and Hamersveld refused to meet her.

Fear tightened her chest.

Grief tunneled through, tossing out worst-case scenarios.

Taking one hand from the wheel, she hit the window button. The glass pane rolled down. Crisp mountain air rushed into the cab, bringing scant relief. She drank in the reprieve anyway, scanning dark shoulders next to graying blacktop, searching for a rest stop. A sign that indicated one. A lookout along the scenic route. A slight widening of the road. Any place, no matter how small, as long it provided a safe place to pull over.

An excellent plan with an obvious problem.

She was in the middle of nowhere. In the dead of night. Driving a stretch of highway cut through the wilderness. Craggy cliffs rolled in endless waves on her right. Thick forest closed her in on the left. Nothing but two lanes of asphalt with faded yellow lines rising and falling with hilly terrain in front of her.

A sharp S-curve swung her around another blind corner.

Her headlights tunneled through the dark, washing through patchy fog. The haze messed with her vision, making her see things that couldn't be there. Wispy swirls looked like ghosts rising in the gloom. Shifting shadows looked wild animals standing on the shoulder of the road. A closer inspection revealed nothing more than crooked tree branches and oddly shaped rocks.

Her imagination didn't care, flagging danger everywhere she looked. The longer she drove, the more tense she became. Fighting to keep the truck on the road, she peered through the brume. Wondering. Waiting. Hoping, wishing, praying she found what she needed around the next bend.

Her stomach bucked again.

Holding on by a thread, she reached for the package of crackers sitting in the passenger seat. Without looking, she pulled three saltines from the plastic sleeve and drove up a steep hill. The truck slanted. Oversized tires hummed across pavement as the engine rumbled. Gaze glued to the top of the rise, she ignored the whining motor, and nibbling on the corner of the cracker, crested the steep hill. Turning the wheel, she swung around the corner.

Tall trees angled into shrubbery. The earth fell away on one side, opening into a specular view of the Pacific Ocean. Faint moonlight fell like raindrops, splashing across undulating waves. As light danced across the surface, painting dark water with sparkling hues, she spotted the place where the road widened ahead.

Relief hit her like a body shot.

Tears pricked the back of her throat.

Finally. A lookout. One without bathrooms but…

Who cared?

Fenced in by high guardrails, the cutout gave her a safe place to—

Tingles swept her spine.

Awareness cut through the chaotic clang of mental noise. Her terror, all the raging uncertainty, disappeared as a low growl echoed. Butterflies took flight in her belly. Her breath caught. Her stomach settled as heightened sensation swirled

across her temples, soothing frayed nerves. Disbelief dropped away. The tears she refused to let fall
for weeks tipped over her bottom lashes.

This was it. It must be it. *It had to be it.*

Hamersveld was here. He must be close. Able
to sense her and—

A link opened up, then expanded inside her
head.

"Natalie," a deep voice murmured, aggression
in the undertone. *"I warned you, baby. I warned
you what would happen if you returned."*

"Thank God," she whispered, clinging to the
sound of him like a lifeline. Peering out the windshield, she eased her foot off the gas pedal. "Thank
God. Please…where are you? Where—"

"Here."

The snarl streamed over the hood.

The truck bucked as Hamersveld uncloaked
overtop of the road. Blown from the clifftop, shale
rumbled down the rock-face. Treetops thrashed in
the blowback. The ocean reacted to the vicious
vibe, kicking up in the presence of a water dragon.

Whispering his name, she took her hands from
the wheel and reached for him. The backend of the
truck fishtailed. She let it happened, too busy
taking in the beauty of him to care where she
ended up. Shark-gray scales flashed. Huge fangs
gleamed in the dark. Massive talons uncurled and
stretched toward her. Black eyes rimmed by bright
blue met hers through the windshield.

A sob escaped her as sharp claws shrieked
against steel.

The sides of the truck dimpled.

A second later, the F-150's tires left the ground and—

Liftoff.

She closed her eyes as relief streamed into gratefulness. He had a hold of her. After weeks spent worrying, heartsick at the thought of causing him trouble while suffering without him. And yet, just as she hoped, the second she broke through the five-hundred-mile maker, he'd flown out in search of her.

"Sveld."

"You shouldn't have come back, shaleima."

Her mouth curved as he called her "water lily" in Dragonese. The endearment told her all she needed to know. Despite his words, he wasn't angry with her. "I had to. No choice. You need to know that I'm—"

"Fuck." Wind whistling over his wings, he banked hard. The truck swung wide. His talons slipped. With a curse, he tightened his grip on the cab. She jumped as his claws punctured the passenger side door. *"Hang on. Hold on, Natalie."*

"What?" she asked as the flight turned wild. "What is it?"

"Incoming," he said, tone guttural, his Norwegian accent so thick she struggled to understand him. *"Enemy pack. I'm going to—"*

A streak of brown with orange flecked scales materialized out of thin air.

Hamersveld snarled as the enemy dragon hit him broadside.

Claws shrieked against metal as the brutal strike ripped her from her man-dragon's talons.

Hurtled into the open, the truck spun in mid-air. The world tilted out of control. The seatbelt slammed her against the seatback.

Unable to breathe, she yanked the nylon strap pinning her in place. No give. She went after the buckle, hitting the mechanism with the side of her fist. Locked tight. Zero movement across her hips. She looked up and caught a flash of guardrail. Panic slammed through her as she sailed over the cliff edge. Jagged snarls of rock registered. The dark expanse of blue shoreline came into view.

Trapped inside the cab.

Spinning out of control above open water.

No way for her to bail out.

Adrenaline unlocked her lungs. She screamed for Hamersveld. A snarling hiss broke through the link she shared with him. The sound of dragon claws striking scales echoed inside her head. Next, a roar. Then a grunt of pain as the man she loved fought for his life and the F-150 angled into a nosedive, on a collision course with chaotic chop of ocean below.

5

The enemy dragon came out of nowhere, hitting him broadside.

Hamersveld heard his ribs crunch. Pain spiraled. His body whiplashed, ripping Natalie and the F-150 from his talons. Metal shrieked. Disbelief summited a nasty peak as the air left his lungs. Gravity took hold, hurling him into a dead spin, toward thick forest and spiked treetops.

Struggling to breathe, he watched the truck fly out of reach and fought to regain control. Bent at odd angles, half-folded, his wings shot straight out. Shark-gray webbing caught damp air. Agony upped its game, making his shoulder muscles squawk as Natalie's scream echoed across the bluff.

Hearing her fear, he gritted his teeth and flapped his wings. He needed to get back to her. Protect her from the threat. Keep her safe from the water. Kill the asshole who'd attacked him, then retrieve his mate.

Sliver paint flashed as the truck flew over the cliffs.

Natalie cried out again.

Hamersveld snarled in reaction. Primal instinct, his need to protect her, took over. The tilt-a-whirl evened out. His downward spiral stopped. Back in control, he banked into a tight turn and searched the sky. Dark brown scales with iridescent orange flecks flashed in his periphery. Quick reflexes flipped him sideways as the enemy male swiped at him. Arching his spine, he avoided the strike, lashed out with his own claws and—

Clang!

A direct hit.

Dragon blood splashed up his forearm.

Baring his fangs, he spun and hammered the asshole again. The bastard yelped as his brown scales split open. Orange flecks flew off interlocking dragon skin, exploding skyward like confetti and—

Hristos. He recognized his attacker.

Surprise made him pause for an instant. The brutal need to tear the asshole apart shoved it out of the way. Arrogant little prick. Zidane needed his head examined. Or better yet, it ripped off. What in the hell did the pampered prince think he was doing? An excellent question, particularly since the male was an ally of the Razorback pack. Or so Zidane claimed when he landed in Seattle. The prince's actions tonight, though, dispelled that belief.

Hamersveld's gaze narrowed as Zidane lined up another strike. Just as well. He hated the male.

Hadn't liked Rodin's firstborn son in Prague. Liked him even less flying in American skies.

Wings spread wide, wind whistling over his horns, Hamersveld searched for Natalie in the night sky. Her aura glowed bright, beaming out the truck windows as Zidane took a swipe at him. Black claws slashed at his smooth scales. With a fast turn, he avoided the blow and flicked his tail. The sawtooth tip clipped the Zidane's side. More blood. Another curse. He dipped, turned and circled back around.

Citrine gaze aglow, Zidane snarled at him.

Hamersveld rotated into a somersault. His magic pulsed. The clouds opened up. Heavy rain fell, splattered across his bladed spine as he flipped upright and counted off the seconds. Timed his strike. Flying so fast, his gray scales blurred, blending into the storm glow. He dropped the cloaking spell. He didn't need invisibility here. Driving rain camouflaged his movements, hiding him in the weave of surging violence, making it hard for Zidane to track him in the dark.

Lightning forked across the sky.

Natalie called out to him.

Tracking her flight, he sent more magic her way. Heat swirled across cresting waves. The boost slid beneath the truck, keeping her level and out of the water, speeding her across the seascape, away from the battle to a place Zidane's warriors would never—

Tracking her aura, a yellow dragon blasted over the shoreline.

Hamersveld hissed in denial. Goddamn Zidane.

Now he knew why the bastard had come out to play. The prince was after his mate. Unable to waste an opportunity to get his claws on a high-energy female, the prick planned to keep him occupied long enough to abduct Natalie. The speed and direction of the yellow-scale dragon as he blasted over choppy ocean waves was all the proof he required. Which meant he needed to change tact right now. Intercept Zidane's warrior before he reached Natalie, and he lost her forever.

With a roar, he opened a link into mind-speak. *"Ivar!"*

"What the fuck, Sveld? You know better," his friend growled. *"Flying out like a crazy asshole. Leaving us in your dust."*

Ignoring the censure, he snarled, *"How close are you?"*

"Twenty seconds."

"Make it sooner."

"Shit," Ivar said. *"How many Nightfuries in the sky?"*

"No Nightfuries. Zidane."

Silence met his pronouncement. One second ticked into two, then—

"He dares?"

"I've got his blood on my claws, so...yeah. The arrogant prick dares."

A low snarl came through the connection. *"Kill him. Take him apart, piece by fucking piece."*

"No time. My mate's in trouble," he said, watching the yellow dragon close the distance. Less than five hundred meters away from the truck. Too close for comfort. *"I've got to—"*

The enemy's talons brushed the tailgate.

With a curse, Hamersveld unleashed his magic. Power surged across the top of the water. Without him to hold it up, the F-150's grill tilted down. Gravity took over. The front end slammed into rising waves. Steel buckled. Saltwater closed over the cab, dragging Natalie under as the enemy male hovered above the surface of the ocean.

"Jesus, Sveld," Ivar muttered, rocketing into view with a battalion of Razorbacks in tow. *"Get to her, then bug out. The boys and I will handle Zidane."*

Without hesitation, Hamersveld left the battle behind. Gaze glued to the spot his mate disappeared, he blasted over the high cliffs. Sand kicked up as he cut across the beachfront. Water frothed. Waves spiked, stretching skyward to touch him. As the gnarled fingers raked his underbelly, Hamersveld dove into the Pacific.

Cold, wet and dark closed over his scales.

His sawtooth spine sliced through the surf. His water vision sparked. Details jumped into focus. His sonar pinged, providing a map of the underwater topography. Smooth ocean floor transitioned to jagged volcanic rock as he swam out to sea. His webbed paws pulled him forward. The slash of his tail upped the speed, propelling him away from the coast. Flowing over a ridgeline, he rocketed past the continual shelf as headlights flickered once, then went out, engulfing his mate in darkness.

6

The impact threw her forward.

The seatbelt tightened another notch as saltwater slammed into the windshield. The glass cracked. She watched the fissures spread, yanking at the cross-body strap, breathing too fast, feeling the cold rush pour through the open driver side window and drench her clothes.

Panic made her yank harder.

No give. Hardly any room for her to maneuver. The buckle was locked tight, the belt strung even tighter. A one-two punch that immobilized, trapping her inside the cab.

She needed a knife. Something sharp to slice through the nylon strap. If she got loose, she could swim to the surface, stay buoyant in the waves until Hamersveld reached her.

A shadow with wings flew overhead.

She heard a low growl, then a crunch. Something big hit the surface of the water. Yellow scales. Glowing blue eyes. Not Hamersveld. A different dragon. Someone she knew in an instant planned to do her harm.

Cursing through clenched teeth, she struggled harder to break free.

The truck listed sideways.

Metal groaned as quarter panels crumpled, buckling under the pressure.

Terror spun her around the rim of insanity as water touched the bottom of her chin. Fighting the panic, she tilted her head back. She took deep breaths, filling her lungs, trying to store oxygen. Breathe in quick. Exhale fast. In the way of free divers. She needed to be able to hold her breath long enough for—

"Shaleima, hold on."

"Sveld—"

"Give me a second."

A shadowy gray blur sliced past the truck.

The yellow dragon flailed, wings thrashing, fighting to get out of the water.

Heat swirled in. Saltwater poured out of the truck, dropping the level to her chest, then hips and feet. As the cab emptied, a warm pocket of air moved in, acting like an oxygen tank, giving her what she needed to breath as the F-150 leveled out, then bumped down on the ocean floor.

A snarl echoed through the deep.

The sound of claws striking scales drifted. Bones snapped. Someone screamed. Natalie closed her eyes and waited. Any second now. Hamersveld would be back any second now. She sensed him close. Knew he fought to protect her by unleashing his water dragon and chasing his enemy out of the sea. All she needed to do was stay still and breathe. Hold on and wait—no matter how freaked out she felt sitting in the dark, inside a wrecked truck at the bottom of the ocean.

Breathe in.

Breathe out.

Be grateful for the heat along with the oxygen.

Suffering in silence, Natalie tried to be patient. Battled to remain calm instead of give into panic. Any second now. Any moment—

Something raked the side of the truck.

Her eyes popped open. Her head whipped to the side. Black eyes with a glowing rim of bright blue met hers through the window. Relief stole her breath. Tears filled her eyes. His huge talons flexed. Dark blue claws sliced through the steel. The sunroof above her head shattered. Glass exploded outward as he peeled the top of the truck back.

"It's locked," she rasped, yanking at her seatbelt. "I can't…it's locked."

Shark-gray scales shimmered as he flicked his claws. The air shimmered. Compression across her chest loosened. The bubble floated up, liberating her from the confines of the truck.

A sob escaped her. Needing to touch him, she reached out.

"Gonna bring you up, shaleima," he murmured, palming the airlock that provided life-giving oxygen. *"Find a safe spot to set down. Check you out. Make sure you're okay, yeah?"*

Unable to wait that long, she shook her head. "No."

"Natalie—"

"No. I can't wait. I need you right now."

"Baby—"

"Shift. Please, Sveld, shift and get in here."

He hesitated, then did as she asked. Warm water became warmer as he shifted from dragon to human form. She watched talons turn into hands, saw scales smooth into skin and the horns on his head disappear. Any other time, she would've paid attention to his transformation. Not tonight. With desperation driving her, she needed him too much. Wanted to be in his arms with her skin pressed tight to his instead of admiring the view.

"Sveld..."

With a groan, he answered the plea and entered the airlock. Big hands reached for her. She launched herself at him. Her body slammed against his. Wet clothes slid against his naked skin as his arms came around her. Face pressed into his throat, she clutched at him and burrowed deep, desperate for close to become closer.

"Hey...hey...it's okay," he whispered as her hands grasped at him. "I'm here. You're all right."

Drinking in the reassurance, Natalie raised her head. She caught the concern in his eyes, but it wasn't enough. She needed more. Here. Now. No delay. And so, instead of taking a breath, she tunneled her fingers through his hair, leaned forward, and kissed him hard.

Surprise locked his frame. His arms flexed around her.

Taking advantage, she nipped his bottom lip, then invaded his mouth. His taste hit her. Bliss drove need to new heights as he growled and kissed her back. Dragging her t-shirt up, his fingers danced along her back. He caressed her gently, drifting over her skin, worshiping her with his touch. She wiggled, asking for more. Giving her what she wanted, he slipped his hand beneath her waistband and cupped her behind. Callused palm against smooth skin, he drew her deeper into his embrace.

Humming her approval, Natalie broke the kiss long enough to yank her shirt off. Her mouth found his again. He shoved her sweatpants down, then off. Naked in his arms, relief scrambled her molecules, putting her back together one piece at a time as her breasts met his chest. Impatient, needy, so deep in desire she didn't care where she was, she kicked her feet free and swung her legs around his hips.

"Yeah?" he asked, tone guttural, pressing his erection against the heat of her. "Here?"

"And now." Mouth brushing his, she met his gaze. Hunger burned in his, mirroring her own as she rolled her hips, coating him in slickness. "Right now, handsome. Need you."

"Goddess, Natalie. Gorgeous," he groaned, supporting her weight, holding her secure, encouraging her to undulate against him. "Beautiful. Just like that, baby."

"Miss me?"

"So much. So fucking much, *shaleima*. Hungry too. Haven't fed. Couldn't touch another female. Needed you. No one else but you."

"I'm sorry, honey."

Rubbing his cheek against hers, he shook his head. "I'm not…I'm not."

"You feel good."

"You feel better."

She smiled against his mouth. "I'm here now. Take what you need, Sveld. All you need."

Fingers playing in the long strands of her red hair, he kissed her. Soft. Sweet. With so much feeling, he made her love him more, then said, "It's gonna be rough. Waited too long. I can't—"

"Good." Pausing for effect, she nipped his bottom lip. He tensed. She licked over the sting. "Fuck me hard. Fuck me quick. We'll save slow for another time."

He didn't hesitate to swing her around.

Her back touched down on the floor of the airlock.

Holding on tight, she opened for him. He found her fast and thrust deep. Pleasure spiked. Bliss spiraled. Ecstasy stole her mind, arching her spine, tilting her hips as he powered in, retreated and came back to her. Skin sliding over skin. Heat meeting heat. Mind-blowing beauty. Perfection made manifest. Exactly how she wanted to be ridden by him—hard and fast, the power of their connection blazing as he loved her tough, making her beg for more.

7

F loating inside an air bubble at the bottom of the ocean, Hamersveld tried to lift his head. A no-go. He was too relaxed. Body lax. Magic humming. Muscles and limbs uncooperative, so sated his mind refused to come back online.

Content to stay right where he was, he burrowed deeper, maintaining the connection, determined to stay buried inside his female for as long as possible. Sprawled on top of him, head tucked beneath his chin, knees bent, thighs snug against his hips, Natalie mumbled something incoherent and snuggled closer. He tightened his arms around her, cuddling her back as pleasure rose in the drift.

Gratitude followed, tightening his throat.

Two months without her. Eight weeks plagued by regret. Long days filled with heartache. Longer nights as he went nine rounds with self-loathing, unable to believe he'd let her go. He spent those desperate hours replaying the reasons—her safety first among them.

Selfish to keep her.

Devastating to let her leave.

Most males would've gone the selfish route, refusing to release her into the wilds of human society. No matter the pain, he'd put her first, forced her to go, unable cage and keep her. He hadn't been able to live with the consequences. Then and now. Couldn't watch her suffer under the yoke of Dragonkind—a culture that was often cruel to women. Especially ones of Natalie's caliber, a high-energy female with an unprecedented connection to the Meridian.

Plugged directly into the source that nourished all living things, Natalie was unique. A rare pearl hidden in the midst of precious gems.

Males of his kind would kill to meet her, never mind mate her. The fact she trusted him enough to rest easy in his arms humbled him. She should be miles away. Safe from him and the curse of his kind. He'd suffered to make sure it happened, except...

She'd come back. Driven straight into his territory knowing he'd sensed her. Doing the one thing he warned her never to do. And yet here she lay, flying in the face of his need to protect her.

The turn of events baffled him. Her actions made little sense. She should be miles away. Building a good life for herself far from Seattle. Not here, in his arms, lazing about with him on the bottom of the ocean floor.

She needed her ass tanned...and her head examined.

It wasn't safe. The world he inhabited would

use her for its own purposes. Chew her up, then spit her out.

"Stop it," she whispered, interrupting his turbulent thoughts. "I'm fine. We're good. Don't go catastrophizing."

He frowned. "Catastrophizing? Is that even a word?"

"Do you understand what I mean?"

"Yeah."

"Then who cares."

He huffed in amusement.

Setting her small hands on his chest, she pushed upright. Still buried inside her, he hummed and palmed her hips as she settled astride him. With a practiced move, she brushed her hair over her shoulders, gifting him with the sight of her beauty, and looked at him. "You done freaking out?"

"Not freaking out, *shaleima*."

She arched a brow in disbelief.

"Okay, maybe a little." Fascinated by her hair, he fiddled with the ends, exploring the texture, enjoying the softness. Unable to help himself, he gathered it in one hand, tugged the thick mass over one of her shoulders, and wrapped the fiery strands around his fingertips. "Why'd you come back?"

Green eyes riveted to his, she stared at him, giving nothing away.

"Told you not to, baby," he murmured, fear for her rising. "It's not safe. I'm not safe for you."

"That's a load of bull. You're the safest place for me to be."

"Natalie—"

"I left under duress, with fear riding me hard. I didn't want to go…to leave you… remember?"

His chest tightened. "I remember."

"The universe works in weird and wonderful ways," she whispered.

Confused by the cryptic comment, he scowled at her.

Her mouth curved. "Notice anything different about me?"

He opened his mouth to say no. She was as beautiful as ever. Luminous skin. Curvy body. Pretty face. Lovely hair. Gorgeous jade green eyes. A scent dominated by the perfume of water lilies. Fresh and pure, as wonderous as the woman who possessed it.

Needing more of it, he breathed her in and froze. His brow furrowed. Something was different. Something had changed. Dragon senses searching for the reason, he stared at her. She waited as magic rose like a wave inside him. Energy-fuse, the magical bond between mates, tightened its grip. Her aura flared. The unique bio-energy she threw off like a beacon nearly blinded him, but he refused to look away, mining the connection, hunting for the truth and—

"*Hristos.*" Shock battered him, swamping him under a wave of emotion. "You're…you're…"

"Yes," she whispered. "I am."

Hamersveld opened his mouth.

No sound came out.

He closed it again, then shook his head, battled through the shock, and found his voice. "How? I don't understand…how?"

"How?" Cupping his cheek, she smiled. "Handsome, we had so much sex that day, you could've gotten me pregnant ten times over."

"That's not it. That's not what I mean."

She stilled atop him. "What do you mean?"

"I've tried, Natalie. I've tried to have a son for years. Each time the Meridian realigns I take a female to my bed. Twice a year for centuries, hoping it would happen, but it never did," he said, trying and failing to solve the mystery. "I want children. I want a family. I want someone to call my own. But after so much trying without a single success, I thought…"

He trailed off.

Natalie picked up the slack. "That what—you're infertile?"

Unable to say it out loud, he nodded.

"You're not infertile, handsome. You may have been with those other women, but you aren't with me."

Her words registered. Acceptance came slower, moving understanding along at a snail's pace.

Throat so tight he could barely speak, he whispered, "You're pregnant."

"One-hundred percent knocked up."

Knocked up.

Fucking hell.

His mate was *pregnant*.

Disbelief ravaged him. Elation elbowed it out of the way. Her scent didn't lie. Neither did her bio-energy. A quick exploration of her lifeforce provided clear evidence. His dragon half sensed it.

Smelled it. Accepted it in as true as Hamersveld palmed her hips. Natalie gasped as he flipped her over. The exterior walls of the airlock undulated, sending blue light tumbling across the ocean floor.

A school of fish switched direction. Two hammerhead sharks banked hard, powerful tails pushing saltwater in his direction. Dirt swirled. Pebbles bounced off the bubble as he flattened his hand against her abdomen.

A pulse throbbed deep inside her womb.

Wonder struck. Joy joined the parade, stealing his breath, pushing tears into his eyes. Unable to hold himself upright, Hamersveld folded forward. Cheek pressed to her belly, he nestled in, listening to his child's heartbeat.

Proof of life.

The most beautiful thing he'd ever heard.

A battered sound left his throat. "*Shaleima*...a baby."

Sliding her hands into his hair, she held him to her. "Yeah, honey...a baby."

"You came back to gift me with a child. To make me a sire."

"I came back because I love you," she said, her voice thick with emotion. "Sharing a baby with you is a bonus."

His breath hitched.

"Look at me." Putting on pressure, she tried to pull him away from her belly. "Please, handsome...look at me."

Tears in his eyes, he nuzzled her belly. Kissing her softly, he resisted her pull, lingering in wonderment. So precious. On her own, Natalie was more than he deserved. Carrying his child, she became everything. *Gave him everything.* Her love and trust. His purpose and future. She tugged again. He lifted his head, but kept his hand on her skin, claiming the space between her hipbones.

As his gaze met hers, he dropped his guard and let her in. Let her see everything he felt for her.

Her face softened. "Happy?"

"Thank you," he said, his chest so tight it ached. "Thank you."

"Love me?" she asked, teasing him to lighten the mood.

"More than you'll ever know," he said, embracing heavy emotion, staying in the moment. It was too beautiful to do otherwise. Too important. Too much of everything he'd ever wanted, but believed he'd never have. A female to love. A child to nurture. A family to build. A life to share with those he cared most about in the world. "I love you, Natalie."

A tear fell from the corner of her eye. "No more talk of me leaving, then."

He shook his head. "You're here to stay."

"I am, so time to take me home."

"The cabin?"

"Home is wherever you are, Sveld." Tracing his cheekbone with her fingertips, she nourished him, replenished him, feeding him with her touch. "As long as I'm with you, I'm good."

He'd make sure of it. Kill and maim, battle his demons and threats from others to ensure she stayed safe, happy, and healthy.

Dipping his head, he kissed her belly, then

drifted up her body. A gentle touch to each hip-bone. One pressed to the spot between her breasts. Worshiping her. Loving her. Showing her how much as his mouth moved on her. She shifted in welcome beneath him. Humming, he licked over her nipple, sucked on the pebbled peak, then turned his head to bathe the other.

She made a needy sound.

He nipped her gently. Kissed her softly, licking the small sting away. She moaned. Hamersveld growled and increased the pressure. As she arched, he slid his hand between her thighs and played in her slick folds, deepening her pleasure, feeding his own.

"Sveld."

"Round two, *shaleima*." Stroking her clit, he sucked harder. "Gonna love you slow and sweet before I take you home."

Chasing an orgasm, she cupped the back of his head. "Perfect."

Wasn't it, though?

Perfect in every way. The absolute best. More than he ever hoped for, a dream come true, made even better by the fact it was right. Right time. Right place. Right female. Finally. At last. After decades spent alone in the dark, he'd found heaven...and its name, surprising as it seemed, was Natalie.

Grab your copy of FURY OF CONVICTION here and read all about how Hamersveld and Natalie first met.

THE NIGHTFURY PACK

VIGNETTES

PRETTY LITTLE PRANKSTERS

Popping the handle, J.J. pushed the Denali's heavy door wide. A quick hop, and her boots crunched down, disturbing the gravel in Black Diamond's driveway—the lair she now shared with Wick and...oh yeah, her shopaholic sister.

Afternoon sun warming the backs of her shoulders, she sighed. Home at last. Finally. After hours spent in expensive shops, under Tania's exacting eye. Now she owned, well...everything. A complete wardrobe underpinned by gorgeous lingerie and—ahem, a few interesting toys from *The Sexy Bandit*—sex shop extraordinaire.

J.J. shook her head. Talk about an eye-opener. A lot more of an education than she needed, too.

Stepping around the back bumper, J.J. glanced at her sister as Tania stopped alongside her. With a quick flick, her sister popped the back of the SUV open. Hinges hissed, lifting the tailgate, showing off the mountain of boxes and bags, designer names plastered across plastic and paper. Her lips twitched. Never let it be said her sister didn't know how to do it up in style. She went for the best of the best. Money? Pasha—no object. Especially while lingerie shopping. Her gaze cut to the Le Cirque bag done up in pretty pink ribbons. Fatigue disappeared, buzzing into full-blown excitement.

Lace and satin. Barely there underthings designed for one purpose—sexual conquest under the guise of fancy ribbons and bows.

Anticipation bloomed, and J.J. hummed. God help her, but she could hardly wait. Wanted to slip into the sexy black number she'd bought right now and blow Wick's mind.

Tania threw her a sidelong glance. "He's gonna love it. Although, you probably won't get to wear any of it very long."

J.J.'s mouth curved. "That's the plan."

A good one too considering Wick couldn't keep his hands off her.

Incredible in more ways than one. Especially since the man-dragon she called mate never said much and reached out even less. Wick wasn't the touchy-feely type...except when it came to her. Thank God and all his angels too. She loved that he wanted her so badly. That he couldn't get enough and made love to her every chance he got. Often where he found her and—

Memories of the morning's romp streamed into her mind.

Heat flared, then burned across her cheeks. She bit the inside of her lip to keep from smiling. Talk about insatiable. He hadn't been able to wait. She hadn't bothered to dissuade him, allowing him to pull her into the laundry room behind him. Which ended in, well…a wicked amount of WOW.

"Your sex kitten is showing," Tania said, amusement in her tone.

"And what?" J.J. raised a brow. "Yours isn't?"

"No question. I can't get enough of Mac either."

"TMI."

Her sister snorted, reached out, and grabbed bags in both hands. "Let's go. Myst and Angela will be waiting to see all our goodies."

"Do you think they'll like what we—"

"They'll love it all," her sister said, turning toward the door. "You can't go wrong with a Taser when Angela's involved. And Myst loves silk and lace as much as I do, so…" Tania grinned over her shoulder. "We're covered."

Covered. Well, that was one way of looking at it. A better way would be *uncovered*, considering all the skimpy *silk and lace* packed behind tissue paper and plastic.

The thought tickled her funny bone.

J.J. huffed, then reached out and snagged her share of the bags. With a tug, she lifted the loot and turned to follow her sister down the flagstone path. Black Diamond's front door stood sentry ahead, a cedar paneled monstrosity that represented change. Huge ones—at least, for her—considering she'd called prison home a month ago. Her chest constricted, making her heart ache and her throat go tight. It always did when she thought about her new home. God, she was lucky. Incredibly grateful too. For Wick, and the life he'd given her. For freedom and safety inside a place where everyone accepted her...

No questions asked. No judgment or rehashing of the past either.

Jogging up the steps behind her sister, J.J. crossed the threshold into Black Diamond's foyer. Silence reigned, telling her most of the warriors were still asleep. Excellent. Perfect, really...particularly since it meant Wick would still be in bed—warm, willing and waiting for her.

A shiver of pleasure rolled down her spine.

With a hum, J.J. upped the pace. Dimmed down halogens glowed overhead, throwing shadows against pale walls as she listened to Tania's high heels ring against slate floor tiles. A sharp right, and Tania entered the first corridor that led to Black Diamond's kitchen. Good idea. The scent of something sweet hung in the air, telling J.J. all she needed to know. Daimler was about to up her caloric intake for the day by plying her with chocolate cupcakes. Or whatever diabolic desert he'd devised to tempt her into—

"Shhh!"

A streak of movement flashed up ahead.

A second later, Angela slid to a stop on sock feet. Red hair gleaming, a can of whip cream in her hand, the ex-SPD detective eyed them from the end of the corridor. Tania flinched and stopped short in front of her. J.J. dodged right. Her elbow smacked into the wainscoting. Bone met wood, sending pain zinging up her arm. Rubbing the sore spot, J.J. threw Angela an incredulous look.

Head on a swivel, acting like a covert commando, Angela checked behind her. "Tania, take those boots off. They're too noisy."

Angela's tone put J.J. on high alert. "What going on?"

Unzipping Gucci's finest, Tania tugged a black knee-high boot off, then attacked the other.

An unholy light in her eyes, Angela grinned. "We got him this time. He's totally screwed."

"Who?" J.J. dropped the bags. Plastic crunched in protest.

"Venom." Mischief gleaming in her eyes, Angela shook the can of Reddi-wip. The clicky-click-click of the nozzle bounced off white walls as she glanced over her shoulder. "You got the feather, Myst?"

Out of breath, Myst skidded to a halt behind Angela. "Got it."

J.J. clenched her teeth to keep from laughing. Uh-oh...the Terrible Two were up to no good again. Which meant things were about to get interesting. A heck of a lot more fun too.

"Where is he?" J.J. asked, her *get-even-gene* answering the call. She couldn't help it. She loved delivering well-deserved payback. And Venom? Her eyes narrowed. Yeah. You betcha. The guy was due. He'd started the war by pouring honey into Angela's favorite Roots boots. So no question, a prank with a crapload of bitch and a cartful of bite was definitely in order. Putting the plans for her lingerie on the back burner, she sidestepped

Tania and jogged toward her friend. "What's the plan?"

Feather in hand, Myst tilted her head to one side. "Come on. And be quiet. We don't want to tip him off."

Oh goody. Sneak attack time.

Hot on her friends' heels, J.J. hightailed it into the kitchen. White cabinets and marble countertops flashed in her periphery. A quick scan and...yup, all clear. Daimler was nowhere in sight. Good thing too. The elf took protecting his "boys" to new heights. If he got wind of Angela and Myst's plan, he'd shut Operation Get Even down faster than she could say *pretty please*. Bypassing the center island, she tiptoed beneath the timber-beamed archway, made a sharp left in front of the monstrosity Daimler liked to call a table, crept into the living room and—

Stopped short.

"Oh, man," she murmured.

"Too perfect," Tania said, right behind her.

And it was. *Way too perfect.*

Eyes closed, blond hair aglow in the lowlight, head resting against the couch-back, Venom sat at one end of the large sectional. His slouch said re-laxed. The soft snore said fast asleep. The open book—facedown and spine up—on his chest said...

J.J. frowned.

Well, she didn't know what the book said about the guy. She read the title again—Idiot's Guide to Power Yoga. She smothered a snort. Re-ally? Venom was into *yoga*? Not exactly what she expected from a bad-ass. Then again, not much inside Black Diamond ever landed inside the realm of expectation.

Not with a pack of dragon-shifters in residence.

Circling around behind him, Angela popped the top on the Reddi-wip, hovered the nozzle above his open hand, and…oh baby. They had lift off. Whip cream streamed into a pretty curl, building into a fluffy coil in the middle of Venom's palm. Ready to deploy phase two—the tickle-SPLAT…hand-to-face method—Myst raised the feather. A second before, her friend touched his temple, inspiration struck like a lightning bolt.

"Psst," J.J. hissed to get her friend's attention.

Myst and Angela paused mid-prank and glanced her way. J.J. held up one finger, asking the pair to wait, and slipping in between the couch and the coffee table, slid to a stop in front of Venom. Long jean-clad legs stretched out, making his boots the perfect target. Hitting her haunches beside his feet, she picked at the laces until both bows let go. Angela gave her two thumbs up. Myst grinned like a lunatic as Tania snorted in laughter behind her. Nimble fingers working fast, J.J. retied the inside laces. Done tethering his ankles together, she made a quick about-face and headed for relative safety in front of the stone fireplace.

Myst unleashed the feather. Venom's brows collided. She tickled him again. He shifted in his sleep, raised his hand and—

Splat!

Sound echoed. Whip cream exploded across

his face. With a roar, Venom shot to his feet. The book went flying. Pages flapped in mid-air as the laces pulled, yanking his ankles together, unbalancing him. Angela shouted in triumph. As the war cry echoed against the vaulted ceiling, he backpedaled and…

The backs of his knees hit the front of couch.

Momentum threw him backward, launching him over the cushions. J.J.'s mouth fell open. He collided with the backrest and flipped up and over. Arms and legs tangled, he teetered a moment, then disappeared from view, landing with a bone-jarring crash behind the sectional.

"Goddamn it," he snarled from his prone position on the floor. A pause and then, "Angela!"

"Gotcha," the ex-cop yelled, already on the move toward the nearest exit.

"Go, go, go," Myst said, voice ringing out like a battle commander.

J.J. didn't hesitate. Or wait for Venom to get up.

Spinning on the balls of her feet, she grabbed a hold of her sister. A death grip on her hand, she hauled ass, and dragging Tania in her wake, raced around the corner into the kitchen.

Another nasty thump rolled out of the living room.

Venom cursed. Angela hooted in laugher.

"Well played, ladies," he growled, raising the fine hairs on her nape. "Game on."

The warning should've concerned her. J.J. high-fived her friends instead, 'cause…

Oh yeah. Mission accomplished.

Venom – 0. Girl Power Posse – 1.

Crazy satisfying. Wicked fun too. So only one thing left to do. Celebrate the victory in style. Which…without a shadow of doubt…involved finding Wick and putting her fancy new lingerie to work.

FIGHT CLUB
WICK IN THE WIND

"Goddamn it, Sloan! Get the hell out of there before—" The explosion cut Venom off. The concussive *boom!* ripped through the frigid air, blowing him back past a row of parked dump trucks. Ravenous flames followed, lighting up the night sky, blistering yellow industrial-grade paint and melting steel like ice cream in the noonday sun.

Perfect. Just what he didn't need. Wick on the rampage.

Flipping guy. Trust the male to come in hot, hammer the enemy while threading the needle between his comrades with a nasty exhale. His best friend needed his head examined. Or a serious boot to the ass. Venom couldn't decide, but either option would do. Maybe then Wick would exercise some caution and use the gray matter between his ears. Of which, he possessed a considerable amount...

Under normal circumstances.

Tonight, though, didn't qualify as *normal*.

The Razorbacks had tried to take one of their own—a female who belonged to a member of their pack. Why Wick cared was anyone's guess. The male hardly ever talked, even to Venom, so yeah, it was a crapshoot. One big "what the hell's he thinking now." Not that anyone gave a damn at the moment. The Nightfury warriors were too busy, 100 percent dialed in and on the warpath, chasing the rogues back into the city, away from Mac and his injured mate.

The target had been a natural one. High-energy females always were for the bastards. And no wonder. Rarer than four leaf clovers, women who drew pure power from the Meridian—the source that fed Dragonkind and kept them alive—were valuable. Which meant the war raging between Nightfury and Razorback had reached new heights.

Escalation to the nth degree.

And Ivar, leader of the Razorbacks, was to blame.

The bastard kept crossing the line. He shamed Dragonkind at every turn, targeting H-E females, imprisoning them inside his lair, conducting scientific experiments designed to…

Hell, Venom didn't know exactly. But whatever the nutbar's end game, it couldn't be good. Especially considering the fact he called his pet project a *breeding program*. Jesus, the asshole was hurting females…innocents in a world that preached honor, discipline and the protection of those weaker than themselves.

The thought of what Ivar planned made Venom cringe. Then again, so did Wick.

Equal parts vicious and crazy, his best friend was uncontrollable. A casualty of his upbringing, Wick's rage ran hot, neck and neck with the death wish he carried around like luggage. Venom understood his friend's propensity for violence. Encouraged it even, at least in battle. But sometimes his intensity got to Venom. Made him sad on a soul deep level he found difficult to ignore. Especially since the compulsion had nothing to do with right and wrong, never mind honor or duty. What drove Wick went deeper than that, and like it or not, Venom couldn't do anything to help him.

He'd been there, tried everything he could think of...to no avail.

With a curse, Venom extended his wings, slowing his freefall toward cracked concrete and twisted steel. Air caught in the webbing, and his muscles squawked, stretching under the strain. Good thing he was armored up and buttoned down. His dragon scales were doing their job, making him fire retardant. Convenient, really, cuz yup... the flames were gathering speed, heading toward the shoulder of the road.

Oh, so not advisable.

A forest fire would bring the humans running. They'd call in air support along with cops, forest rangers and firefighters. And a crowd wasn't something Venom wanted, never mind could afford. Not with the rogues in full retreat, desperate to find a way out, one Venom refused to hand them by sending up a giant smoke signal to human authorities.

One eye on the sky, the other on the inferno,

Venom banked hard, his wingtip inches from the ground, and breathed out. A luminous green wave shot from between his fangs, frothing over broken asphalt, stealing the air to douse the flames. Smoke billowed, throwing the smell of burnt rubber and sweet grass up to meet moonlight.

Mission accomplished. No firefighters required.

Now for the Razorback jackoffs dogging his tail. Or rather, on his radar. His sonar pinged, picking up movement over the forest. Ah, hell. Not again. The buggers were playing hide and seek, hop-scotching across rough terrain, hightailing it back to the city in the hopes of losing the Night-fury warriors somewhere along the way.

Losing the enemies' signal in the smoke, Venom fired up mind-speak. *"Wick."*

A yellow Razorback streaked over the ripped-to-shreds asphalt.

Right on the rogue's tail, Wick's black amber-tipped scales flashed in the gloom. *"What?"*

"Holster the fireworks, will yah? I'm in the target zone."

"Well, get the fuck out of there," Wick said, his tone all *Elementary, my dear Watson.* *"I'll smoke the rest out."*

"Give me a minute."

"You got thirty-seconds before I unleash."

Terrific. His buddy was a flipping peach. *"Remind me to kick your ass when we get home."*

"Right," Wick said, anticipation in his tone.

Flipping into a somersault, Venom flew over a downed crane to scan the gully on the opposite side of the highway. Piled up like broken Tonka toys, the steel carcasses, tires still alight and smoking, littered the bottom of the ravine. Hmm...good cover down there. A nice place to hide if a rogue felt so inclined.

Venom rounded the end of a downed dump truck and...bingo. He spotted the Razorback within seconds. Bright blue scales smeared with motor oil, eyes trained on the sky, the male crouched like a cat, no doubt waiting to blow him to kingdom come when he flew over. Venom snorted, a load of "you gotta be kidding me" making the rounds inside his head.

He sighed instead, and angling his wings, changed course. Slithering in on a slow glide, he snarled at the male, startling the idiot. The enemy dragon jumped like a jackrabbit then dodged to avoid his razor-sharp claws. Too late. Venom struck, grabbing the bastard by the tail. Sharp spikes sliced the palm of his talon. He ignored the pain and yanked. A quick flip. A sickening twist and...crack! He snapped the rogue's neck, leaving his ashes to float above blackened field grass.

Using the roof of a backhoe as a launch pad, Venom leapt skyward. He had five seconds before Wick exhaled and—

A flash exploded through the darkness.

"Jesus H. Christ," Sloan growled, catching Venoms' updraft as he cleared the tops of ancient redwoods hugging the stretch of blacktop.

Venom growled as round two rolled in. Blue-orange flame streaked over the treetops, a horrific whistling sound in its wake. Heat went cataclysmic, sucking the oxygen from Venom's lungs. Choking on the smell of sulfur, he tucked his wings and rocketed into a tight spiral. The fireball roared past, singeing his scales, missing him by inches. He counted off the seconds, eager to see what Wick's arsenal unearthed. Three. Two. One…

The ravenous fireball struck.

Sound boomed, warping perception as shock waves expanded into a brutal surge. Newly poured concrete buckled then heaved, erupting skyward, as the lava encased inside Wick's fireball splattered in all directions. Enemy dragons screamed, abandoning their hidey-holes behind hapless graders and industrial-sized bulldozers.

Venom almost snarled in satisfaction, then thought better of it. No need to get cocky. He wasn't out of the woods yet. Especially with Wick unleashed and on the loose.

THE SCREAMING NEVER GOT OLD. Neither did the pain. Oh, the sweet, sweet sound of pain: held high on midnight air, emerging from enemy throats, the violent clicking of scales and flapping wings. The stink of desperation on bitter wind as the Razorbacks tried to get away. To avoid the wide arcing splatter of Wick's magma-filled exhale.

Deadly. Efficient. Incendiary. A trifecta of nastiness that never failed; a gift that just kept on giving.

Thank fuck.

The chaos was heartwarming. The cause and

effect one Wick relished about the striking ferocity of his arsenal...along with the panic and the confusion he left in his wake. The enemy never saw it coming. Not that he lamented the fact. The chemical complexities of his exhale elevated his game, giving him the advantage in a firefight. Like Jawbreaker candy humans enjoyed sucking on, the fireballs he unleashed had layers: the undeniable sweetness of blue flame on the outside, the ooey-gooey goodness of lava on the inside, a layer of poisonous gas between the two.

Sweet and sour with a hit of hot sauce. Wicked boom-boom factor with a healthy dose of holy shit.

Hot on the tail of a Razorback, Wick banked hard, avoiding the upthrust of a twisted crane boom. Leaving the broken highway and devastation behind, he streaked across the winter-black sky, tracking the enemy, letting them draw him away from comrades and the fighting. Stupid rogues. Thick as thieves, the three stooges meant to slink away...to leave their buddies high and dry, prey to the Nightfury warriors he called brothers.

"Good luck with that," he murmured, sincere in the well-wishing.

And why not? Wishing them luck wouldn't change the facts. Or what would happen to the *Dickless Three* trying to escape him.

Locked on, Wick's gaze narrowed on the enemy males desperate to stay out of range. He wanted to roll his eyes at the futility. He snarled instead, brutality and intent melding in his low growl. It was only fair. The rogues he pursued over thick forest deserved the warning. Did it matter that they didn't stand a chance? That giving the Razorback posse a head start, and a head's up, wouldn't spare them in the end? Nah, not really.

Nothing and no one would save them.

Not with him on their trail.

Inevitable was, after all, just that—*inevitable*. Unavoidable…whatever. Choose the adjective, whatever one worked. Each male had sealed his fate the instant the rogue pack attacked his brothers-in-arms. So yippee, roll out the red carpet. Let the flash of fireballs fly. Payback was a bitch, and the rogues would end up where each belonged— dead and gone, nothing but ash drifting on a winter-fed breeze in the middle of nowhere.

Good thing the enemy hadn't realized it yet.

The Razorbacks still thought they had a chance of evading him. Perfect. He didn't want them to turn belly up and beg for mercy. Where, after all, was the fun in that? No chase equaled zero satisfaction. Not something Wick wanted to entertain. He needed the challenge. Loved the hunt. Thrived in battle and the brutal place every fight took him —back to the core of who and what he was…

A natural born killer.

Night vision pinpoint sharp, his golden eyes glowed, throwing yellow light out to illuminate the darkness. Enemy scales glimmered up ahead. Satisfaction spiked as Wick's sonar pinged. Sensation curled around his horns, making his scales tingle. Almost there, but he couldn't unleash…

Not yet.

He needed to time his attack. Make certain he

struck at the precise moment. Otherwise, he wouldn't get what he needed.

Rogue blood coating his talons. More dead Razorbacks to add to his running tally.

Gritting upper fangs into lower, he wound his magic tight, forcing the gathering power to chase its tail. Incendiary, the brutal swell built into a lethal force, frothing at the rim of his control. The instant it boiled over Wick tossed it like dice. The death-dealing wave slithered on chilly air, then whiplashed, blanketing the rough terrain. Trace energy bounced back, bringing information along with it.

Wick's lip curled, exposing one of his fangs. Excellent. The idiots were in the pipe, all three in the hot seat. If he exhaled now, he'd nail all three, inflict maximum damage with little effort.

A solid plan. No doubt the best course of action, but...

No way would he take the easy way out.

Neat and tidy wasn't his thing. Wick disliked crisp corners and pretty bows on packages. Messy was more his style, which meant he was about to catch hell. Again. Not from the assholes up ahead, but from Venom. His friend wouldn't be pleased. Not with the three-to-one odds, never mind him. He'd want Wick to wait. To fall back and track the rogues while he called for backup.

Wick grunted. *Backup.* Right. Like that was going to happen? No fun lay in that direction, just more of the same. Boredom with a slap-happy helping of zero challenge. Venom accused him of having a death wish. Maybe his friend was right.

Maybe not, but whatever the case, the whys and wherefores weren't important now. All that mattered was that he got what he needed—a ball busting fight, and the release that always accompanied it.

Tucking his wings, Wick rocketed between two huge pines. Rocky outcroppings grew into high bluffs, reaching jagged hands toward shrouded skies. His sonar pinged again. He zeroed in, flying toward the cliffs, herding the rogues ahead of him. Close. He was close now and gaining fast, a mere football field from the tip of the lead dragon's tail.

With a growl, Wick increased his wing speed. His velocity moved from oh-my-God fast to holy shit supersonic. Wind whistled over his scales, sound whirling out to touch enemy ears. The rogues reacted, changing course like a flock of panicked geese. Frosty air rolled into his throat as he breathed deep, filling his lungs to capacity. Fire grew, feeding on oxygen as lava flowed into the back of his throat. A dangerous cocktail, poisonous gas joined the party, marrying magma with flame.

Exhaling hard, Wick unleashed, aiming left of center. The fireball rocketed between his fangs and—

Slam!

Oh, baby. Bull's-eye. Right on target.

Wick grinned as the cliff side exploded. Rock and molten spray shot fifty feet into the air. Razorbacks squawked. Hmm, yeah. Lovely. The pricks were 100 percent predictable. And now headed exactly where he wanted them to go... into the open-pit mine abandoned by humans over a decade ago. Deep and wide, the quarry's mouth gaped, the striated walls spiraling toward damp earth and into dark corners. Fine by him. The deeper the hole, the better Wick liked it. Especially if it took him into the bowels of the Earth, allowing him to curl up next to lava flow and—

"Wick." The deep voice came through mindspeak. *"Give us your twenty."*

Wick clenched his teeth. Fucking Sloan. The male had the worst timing, piping in when least expected. Interrupting his grove, interfering with a triple kill on the horizon.

Just what he didn't need.

Too bad he was about to get a face-full of the male.

Sloan might not be able to triangulate his exact position, but Venom could. His best friend knew him like no other. Venom fought with him night after night and was hooked into the unique energy signal that curled from his wing-tips like gas fumes. Which meant he had a minute—maybe three, tops—before his packmate entered the fray and screwed with his mojo.

"I'm so kicking your ass."

Ah, speak of the devil. Pain in the ass best friend officially in the house.

"Fuck off," Wick said, relying on his favorite two words. *"I've got 'em cornered."*

Sloan cursed. *"Ah, come on, man—share."*

"No." Sharing wasn't an option. Not tonight. Less than twenty yards away, the enemy was almost in range. Another few seconds and he'd en-

gage, rattle the rogues' cages with a shitload of down and dirty. *"Go find your own playmates."*

"KO'd them all," Venom said through clenched teeth. *"How many you got in the pipe?"*

"Three."

"Crazy son of a bitch," Sloan murmured.

"Goddamn it, Wick. We're thirty seconds out. Wait until we get there."

The worry in Venom's voice cranked Wick tight. He hated that tone, the one that said *be reasonable.* Why? Every time his friend used it, he knew he was right. Waiting was smarter, the safer bet all the way around. But he couldn't do it. He needed the burn of release, the calming effect killing the enemy would bring. Sad? Absolutely. True? Undeniably. Venom recognized it, and so did Wick. His sickness went soul deep, turning his insides black, egging him on, building the pressure inside his skull until reason stepped aside and compulsion took over. Until he lost himself in the ugly swirl of impulse and aggression.

So yeah, as much as he disliked causing his friend to worry, he was going in. Maybe then, he'd be able to sleep when he got home.

Focus razor-sharp and narrowed on his prey, Wick streaked over the lip of the quarry. Within seconds, he closed the distance and, claws deployed, grabbed the yellow dragon's tail. Knife-like spikes lashed him, slicing his palm wide open. Blood pooled on his skin. Pain streaked up his forearm. Ignoring the discomfort, he yanked.

Taut muscles stretched, setting his side on fire as he dragged the rogue backward. The poison-

elbows. His arm muscles protested the tension. He didn't care. Honed by hardship, he barely felt the discomfort. Pain never bothered him anymore. The piercing, jagged sensation focused him instead. Guilt, however? Shite, that bastard remained front and center, tying a knot behind his breastbone, making it difficult to breathe. He stared at the space between his feet and frowned.

Bloody hell. His mind needed to decide. Open wide or shut down tight. Remember everything or forget completely.

It couldn't do both, and after years of living with questions, he was tired of running from the truth. He wanted answers, some kind of closure, one way or other. Before the mental tug of war tore him apart. Before the agony of living in the hell of not knowing took its toll, and he lost all sense of himself for good.

The glow around window casing intensified.

With a ragged exhale, Forge released his death grip on the sheet and pushed to his feet. Rolling his shoulders, he turned toward the pocket doors on the other side of his room. Both stood wide open, pushed back into the wall, allowing him to see the rocking chair sitting next to a toy bin piled high with stuffed animals. Gaze locked on the wolf with lopsided ears, he stepped around the end of the bed. Time to get a move-on. His son would wake soon and—

"Da!" The call filtered through the doorway. "Da, da, da, da, da."

His mouth curved as the first urgent cry morphed into happy babbling. Feet still moving toward the nursery, Forge glanced over his shoulder at the digital clock sitting on his bedside table. Three-fifty-four PM. Same time, every day. It never failed. Gregor-Mayhem always woke as afternoon lengthened into early evening. Uncanny, a touch freaky, but no real surprise. Dragonkind infants were stronger than human babies—more alert, more aware, faster on the cognitive development and physical fronts too. Toss in the fact a warrior could set his watch by one and...aye. A perfect time piece wrapped in a precious wee package.

"Da!"

"Hold onto yer tail faethers, laddie. I'm coming."

An unhappy squawk answered him.

Dipping his head beneath the door lintel, Forge strode into the room. The space screamed HU-MAN. Human décor. Human superstitions. Human traditions everywhere he looked. Pale blue walls for a boy. A painted-on stencil with kites and bikes and skateboards in place of a chair rail. Winnie the Pooh mobile hanging above the mahogany crib. A shame, to be sure. Miniature dragon skulls bobbing above the crib would've been better than a dumb bear with honey bee issues to entertain his son, but well...

A smart male knew when to keep his mouth shut.

Case in point? His son's given name along with the nursery. Myst—the Nightfury comman-der's mate—was responsible for both. The prissy human set-up didn't bother Forge much. Rooms could be changed—repainted, redesigned, reorganized. No sweat. Hardly any work at all. The human name crammed in front of his son's Dragonkind one, however? Forge grimaced. Almost four months gone, and he still wasn't used to it. Didn't like saying it either. Given half a chance, the "Gregor" part wouldn't exist. He dropped it every chance he got and used *Mayhem*, but only when he was alone. And never with the other Nightfury warriors in earshot.

For good reason—Myst.

The lass loved Mayhem—his full name too, having gifted his son with her Grandda's moniker…the war hero. Forge shook his head while he crossed to the crib. Shite. Of all the rotten luck. Trust a female to tie it up with a neat little bow.

Smart of her. Difficult for him.

Dropping the name came with a formidable problem—hurt feelings on Myst's part. Something he would never cause. He admired her too much to disrespect her in any way. Only a callous fool would hurt the woman responsible for saving his son's life, only to adopt him as her own, so…

The name stayed.

Which meant he must keep his aversion for it under wraps. And adopting the nickname his brothers-in-arms—the other dragon-warriors with whom he shared Black Diamond—used to lessen the gut-punch of a Dragonkind infant with a human name.

"Good morrow, GM. How's my laddie today?" Forge peered over the side of the crib. His gaze landed on the Mohawk first. Rising in the center of his son's small head, the strip of dark hair screamed bad-ass. Already. A sign of things to come. A warrior in waiting. Forge's mouth curved; his heart warming as serious purple eyes met his. Wee feet kicking, blankets in disarray, Mayhem frowned at him. Forge raised a brow. "Hungry, are we?"

Mayhem shoved his fist into his mouth. A suck-suck-sucking sound followed, telling Forge plainer than words what his son wanted. Myst… right now.

"Ma, ma…ma, ma, ma," his son said around his knuckles.

"Yer mam'll be here in a minute."

With a flick, he tossed the baby blanket to one side and picked up his son. His slight weight settled like a gift in his arms. Oh, how he loved this part of the day. The quiet time when he got Mayhem alone. All to himself. No sharing with the female horde who'd invaded the Nightfury lair in recent months. He kissed the top of his head, reveling in the warm bundle as Mayhem snuggled into his chest, laid his cheek against his shoulder and…God. Was there anything better? The closeness and cuddle made him feel needed. Valued. Like an able sire, instead of a fuck up with holes in his memory and heavy guilt in his heart.

His chest went tight, squeezing around his heart.

Forge ignored the awful jab and turned toward

the changing table. "Let's get you a bottle while we wait, shall we?"

"Ba-ba."

"Aye," he murmured against the top of his son's head.

Soft hair brushed his jaw, catching on day old stubble, bringing a soothing wave of steady comfort. The tight knot in the center of his chest loosened. One thread unraveled into more, leaving a messy tangle, but...hell. He didn't care. The reprieve was welcome, a necessary thing to banish the ache in an ocean of nothing but hurt.

Stopping in front of the dresser doubling as a change station, he leaned to one side and tugged the fridge door open. Small, compact, a college sized appliance, perfect for the nursery and the ready-made the baby bottles Myst kept inside it. Grabbing one off the top shelf, he gave it a good shake, then murmured. The beast inside him answered, awakening his dragon half in a rising rush. Magic gathered, then crested, building into an inferno inside him. Pleasure prickled along his skin. Heat bled from his palm. The milky formula warmed inside the glass.

Wee head tucked beneath his chin, Mayhem squirmed in his arms. "Ba-ba."

The perfect temperature now, he shifted his son to the crook of his arm and gave it up. An intense look on his face, Mayhem grabbed the bottle with both hands and stuffed the nipple in his mouth. With a chuckle, Forge laid him on the thick changing pad and reached for a clean diaper. Pajama snaps popped, joining the feeding sounds as he undressed his son and got busy with the clean up. A new diaper went on quick, the clean pair of PJs even faster. Not a moment too soon either. A warm prickle ghosted along his spine. The sizzle rolled toward him, riding the late afternoon air, making the fine hair on his nape stand on end, sounding the alarm.

Almost here. She was just steps away.

Light footfalls sounded outside the door.

A creak drifted through the quiet.

The handle turned. The door swung inward. A slim silhouette stepped in from the hallway and—

"Good eventide, lass."

"Hey, Forge." Blonde hair tumbling over one shoulder, bare feet whispering over wide-planked floorboards, Myst moved deeper into the room. Eyes the color of violets met his, then drifted to Mayhem. "Is he ready?"

"All set."

Gliding to a stop beside him, she leaned in, and with a gentle touch, caressed Mayhem's bare foot. Tiny toes curled, then wiggled as though delighted. Myst smiled, pure joy in her expression. "Hello, beautiful boy."

"Ma...ma, ma, ma." Mayhem grinned around the nipple, greeting Bastian's mate, then went back to sucking.

Mama.

Forge's throat tightened. How incredible. He hadn't dared hope. Had never expected such a welcome turn of events. Not once in the eight months Caroline Van Own carried his child had he dreamed a female might take on the role of mother to his son. He'd made a terrible miscalculation with Caroline. One he couldn't undo or take back. A mistake that could never be forgiven. The moment he realized his error—impregnating her without first ensuring his dragon half had bonded with her—he'd known what it meant.

Certain death for Caroline.

Another female taken in her prime.

Another motherless son in a long line of many.

One hundred percent his fault. A terrible truth to face. A hard thing to admit. The inherent difficulty, however, didn't make it any less true.

Or him any less culpable.

He bathed in shame every day. Flogged himself for doing the unforgivable and taking a human life. For ending Caroline's before it truly began. Not that he'd killed her on purpose. Arrogance played a part in his mistake. Hope and faith as well. The belief he could force the connection—one his kind called *energy-fuse*—to create a lasting bond that would keep her healthy during pregnancy and save her life in the end.

He knew better now.

The universe didn't work that way. Or make exceptions for good intentions. He'd put the cart before the horse. Energy-fuse couldn't be forced. Elusive. Powerful. A magical bond between mates, the connection most males coveted but never managed to find. Dragonkind DNA—the unique energy signature in each warrior's blood—was too finicky for such falsehoods. It recognized truth, ignored denial, matching and marrying the Meridian's energy streams in individuals. One Dragonkind male, one human female who matched his energy frequency down to the decimal and... wham! Harmony times a trillion. Exacting. Uncompromising. Eternal. A match made in magic and the powerful electrostatic bands that ringed the planet, nurturing all living things. Dragonkind included.

No male could fight or fake it.

The knowledge was his cross to bear along with Caroline's death. And yet, even as he mourned her, Forge reveled in Mayhem, rejoicing in the small things: each growth spurt, every new lesson learned and word said. The way his son's Mohawk gleamed in the low light and his dark lashes flickered as he drank from the bottle. The fact Myst now mothered his infant son.

It didn't matter that Myst belonged to another male. Or that she wasn't Mayhem's biological mother. Not for a second. A mother for his son. A woman who loved his child with the whole of her heart was all that mattered. Now. Tomorrow. In the future. Forge couldn't have asked for better for his son.

"God," she whispered, stroking Mayhem's tiny foot again. "He's getting so big."

"Infants do that."

She sighed. "Too fast for my liking."

"You'll have yer own soon enough," he said, glancing at her stomach. Hidden beneath a cotton tee, her belly rounded, growing bigger by the day. Four months along, carrying Bastian's unborn child, and pleased as punch about it. Impending motherhood looked good on Myst. Went together better than sugar in shortbread cookies. He glanced at her sideways. "Another tiny babe to coddle. A playmate for GM."

"I can hardly wait."

"So you keep telling me."

She laughed and laid a hand on her belly. "He started moving yesterday."

"Kicking?"

"Like a pro soccer player. Surprised the heck out of me. Freaked Bastian out a little."

"Aye," he said, remembering the first time Mayhem moved inside Caroline's womb. He'd been so proud, full of anticipation and joy. Before he'd learned he and Caroline weren't meant for one another. Sorrow rose in a grief-filled wave. Forge clenched his teeth to stem the tide of emotion. Stupid. Such hubris. Blatant willfulness driven by intense loneliness. Now he paid the price for his arrogance—Caroline cold in her grave and a conscience that couldn't be wiped clean. "The babe will only grow stronger, Myst. Be sure tae take yer vitamins."

She snorted. "Like I have a choice? Daimler would hold me down and force feed me them if I didn't."

He believed it. The Numbai—the Nightfuries' go-to guy—never took no for an answer. Especially when it came to those he considered his responsibility. "Bastian would help."

"No kidding. I have five months to go, and he's already driving me crazy. I swear to God if Bastian doesn't stop hovering, I'll be forced to take a baseball bat to his head."

Forge chuckled. "A mate's prerogative, lass. He wants you safe."

"I'll give him safe," she grumbled, pure mutiny on her pretty face. Nudging him out of the way with her hip, she scooped Mayhem off the table, and with a quick pivot, walked toward the rocking chair. Wood rockers sighed against the floorboards as she sat and settled in, his son cradled in the crook of her arm. "Just so you know, they're waiting for you."

Forge tensed, his body reacting to the news with a violent flash of heat. Inferno-like pressure burned through his veins. His muscles tightened over his bones. Prickles of unease swept his spine as dread pooled in the pit of his stomach. Fucking hell. He'd almost forgotten what awaited him tonight—the agonizing claw of memory regression. The awful twisting sensation of allowing another into the inner recesses of his mind.

A bad taste washed into his mouth. "Is B already set up?"

Myst nodded. "Rikar's with him."

"Lovely." And in no way good. Fucked up was more like it.

Bastian must be desperate if he'd included *Frosty* on the dance card. With Rikar in on the two-step, the evening promised a holy shite factor Forge knew would cause problems. Not that he didn't trust the Nightfury first in command. Despite their bumpy beginning, Rikar was solid, bighearted when it counted, smart with an extra helping of IQ. A warrior worthy of his respect, but —Christ. Having Bastian root around inside his head was bad enough. But two males with box seats and a prime view of his screwed up mental landscape? Bloody hell, that didn't bode well...

For anyone.

Too bad the desperate-to-remember couldn't be picky.

Forge smothered a grimace. So much for taking it easy tonight. Looked like he'd be in mind-torquing, brain-freeze territory for a rest of the evening.

Flexing his hands to combat his fear, Forge strode toward the exit. "Later, lass."

"Hey, Forge?"

Already at the door, one hand on the handle, he glanced over his shoulder. "Aye?"

Worry in her eyes, Myst met his gaze. "Maybe you should take the evening off. Not push so hard. You don't need to—"

"I do."

She opened her mouth to argue.

"I cannae go on like this, Myst," he said, cutting off her objection. "I need help. I need to know what happened that night—what part I played in it —once and for all."

"Okay, but if you feel the burn, like before— stop." Balls of her feet planted on the floor, she pushed, setting the rocking chair in motion. The chair seesawed. Mayhem cooed, happy with the motion and the contents of his bottle. Myst drilled him with her best I'm-a-nurse-don't-argue-with-me look. "I mean it, Forge. No messing around. Tell Bastian to stop if it becomes too intense. Rome wasn't built in a day, you know."

Forge nodded, agreeing just to agree...and escape. He needed to *escape*. Right now. Before he changed his mind. Before he decided not knowing was better than what he suspected: that he'd failed his family when they'd needed him most. Running —leaving the lair and disappearing—would solve all kinds of problems. The Archguard would stop hunting the Nightfury pack in an effort to assassinate him. Painful memories would remain sealed, the truth lost for all time. And he would stay sane, but—

Forge shook his head and, yanking the door open, stepped into the corridor. He couldn't do it. His conscience refused to let him. He owed his Nightfury brothers-in-arms too much. Each one had accepted him. Drawn him in. Given him purpose and a new best friend in Mac, a water dragon who commanded magic as powerful as his own. Provided him and Mayhem a home, while worming their way into his heart. Now the warriors he fought alongside every night were family, and a male never turned away from those he loved, so...

No way would he turn tail and run. Not from the truth.

The information he possessed was too important to ignore. Or leave buried somewhere inside his head. No matter the cost of his mental stability, he must stay the course and *remember*. Recall all the ugly details to protect his new pack and provide what they needed to take down the Archguard. Rodin and his thugs required killing, and the Dragonkind hierarchy a thorough cleansing. So aye, no matter how painful, dangerous or damaging, he would try. Over and over. Again and again. Even if the mind regression techniques proved too much and obliterated him in the end.

Read more about Forge and his fight to survive in FURY OF SURRENDER.

THANKSGIVING
DRAGONFURY STYLE

H er first foray out of Black Diamond in weeks, and Angela didn't know what to do first: embrace the freedom or curse the sheer volume of choices. An f-bomb made the rounds inside her head. All right, then—swearing it was. And no wonder. Superstores weren't her usual thing. Stakeouts, high-powered rifles, and taking down bad guys? No problem. She could handle that. But as she stood in the middle of a grocery aisle, facing off with a shelf full of pie fillings, she knew she'd lost her mind.

It was the only explanation. Well, that and love.

Yes. Love. Sheer Geronimo! craziness.

The kind that propelled women into unusual feats of stupidity.

Case in point? The fact she felt compelled to bake a pie. A Thanksgiving pumpkin pie, at that. Why? The answer was simple. It started and ended with one guy: Rikar, frost dragon extraordinaire, her mate, the love of her life. Angela scowled at a can with cherries on the label. Freaking guy and his unpredictable sweet tooth. Idiot her and the drive to please him. But whatever. It was what it was, all ridiculousness aside. No changing it, so Better Homes and Gardens here she came.

Blowing out a long breath, Angela reached out, and shoving the apple and cherry flavors aside, grabbed a can of pie filling. As cold metal settled against her palm, sunlight streamed through the windows at the front of the store, kissing the pumpkin stamped on the label. Yup. This was it. The moment of truth. Would she, could she…or better yet, should she?

Pursing her lips, she shifted the can from one hand to the other. After a second of hesitation, Angela shook her head. No way. Not going to happen. Quitting wasn't an option. She was smart enough to figure it out—was a former SPD homicide detective…damn it—so time to armor up and button down. Making a homemade pie for her mate, after all, couldn't be all that hard.

With a flick of her wrist, she tossed the pie filling into the air. Light glinted off the steel lip as the pumpkin label whirled, orange streaking under industrial grade fluorescents. Catching the can mid-flip, she pivoted and, strides even, headed for the frozen food section. She could do it, seemed harmless enough, just a long list of ingredients that needed to be put together and thrown into the oven. A little time, a lot of patience and poof, fait accompli…pie in hand and Rikar happy.

File it under done.

"I mean, really," she murmured, walking past a

display of fancy olive oils. "How difficult can it possibly be?"

Reading through the grocery list inside her head, Angela rounded the end of the aisle. She turned left, boot treads squeaking on the floor and stepped—

Right into the middle of a tug of war.

Over a bag of peanut M&Ms.

"Daimler, for the love of Pete!" A death grip on the chocolate treat, Myst—her new friend and the Nightfury commander's mate—glared at Black Diamond's butler. "Let go or I swear to God—"

"But my lady, it's full of sugar," the Numbai said, pointy ears hidden beneath a traditional golf hat, his expression so sincere Angela's lips twitched. "Candy isn't good for you. You must think of the baby."

"I am thinking of the baby." With a growl, Myst yanked. Yellow plastic crinkled then slid. Daimler yelped as he lost his grip on the package. The instant he did, her friend hid it behind her back, playing keep away, and shuffled backward. "He wants M&Ms. I'm his mother. I should know."

Daimler frowned. "Unborn babies do not—"

"I'll tell Bastian on you," Myst said, threatening him with her mate's wrath.

He harrumphed, then opened his mouth, no doubt to argue.

Angela cut him off. "One package isn't going to hurt her, Daimler."

"Hurt who?" Entering the fray, Tania stopped beside them, five pounds of butter stacked like bricks in her arms. As she dumped her load into Daimler's already overflowing grocery cart, the third member of the female trifecta, now living inside the lair and mated to Mac, met her gaze. Angela raised a brow, asking without words. Tania grinned, answering in an instant. "I'm making shortbread cookies. They're Mac's favorite."

Well, all right then. Mystery solved. She wasn't the only one on the crazy "please her man" tact. Which...phew...made her 100 percent normal.

Tania's focus dropped to the can in her hand. "What are you making?"

"Pumpkin pie." Shy all of a sudden, she shrugged. "Rikar wants one for Thanksgiving."

Momentarily distracted from keeping her candy safe, Myst blinked and swung in her direction. Giving her the once over, her mouth curved. "You're going to bake a...a..."

"Pie." Registering her friend's disbelief, Angela tossed her a dirty look. "What's wrong with that?"

"Nothing." Struggling to keep a straight face, Myst cleared her throat. "But you do realize we're talking about you...a kick-ass never go anywhere without a gun kind of girl?"

"I'm well rounded," Angela murmured, adjusting the Glock concealed under her leather jacket.

"Sure, you are," Myst said, violet eyes sparkling. "You're a regular Martha Stewart... packing heat while—"

"Oh, Lady Angela!" His flair for the dramatic

riding shotgun, Daimler clasped his hands together. His gold front tooth winked as he smiled and bounced on the balls of his feet.

"Wonderful! Such a lovely idea, but…"

Uh-oh. That didn't sound good. Every time Daimler used the word "but" plans changed and culinary chaos followed. In a hurry. Even so, Angela braved the fallout. "But what?"

Leaning forward, the elf plucked the pie filling out of her grip. He set the can on the nearest shelf, then grabbed her hand. A slight tug full of major manipulation later, and she was headed toward the produce section, Myst and Tania in tow.

Eyes bright with excitement, Daimler glanced over his shoulder at her. They blew past the frozen food aisle. "Canned filling will never do. We must get a real pumpkin. Make everything from scratch. I will teach you how."

God help her. She was in so much trouble. Way over her head with a culinary wizard who didn't understand her limitations in a kitchen. Making dessert from scratch, after all, was light years from pouring ready-made filling into a frozen pie shell. But as Daimler stopped in front of a wooden bin full of pumpkins and said, "pick one, my lady", Angela didn't have the heart to disappoint him. He was past the point of no return. And she was so screwed, 'cause yeah…

Love and pumpkins. Cinderella had nothing on her.

THE SCOTTISH PACK ATTACK

My Writing Lair: July 17, 2023 - 11:42 PM

I'm not a night owl, but staying up past midnight happens sometimes. Tonight is one of those nights. I blame John Wick. *JW 4* has me glued to my screen, headphones of the Princess Leia bun variety covering my ears, making the outside world go still. My internal world, though, is picking up threads, watching the action, cataloguing John's moves, feeding interesting tidbits to my imagination like a zookeeper does a carnivore.

It's a carnival. A balancing act, keeping my appetite for stories well-fed, but as the pieces start to settle (and John picks up a gun), I notice something strange. The light at the top of my screen blinks twice, then stays on. Red dot instead of black spot. A clear sign the camera on my laptop has been engaged—without my permission.

I should be creeped out. I should find a sticky note and slap it over the lens. Or turn the Wi-Fi off.

A couple of clicks will do it, but instead of freaking out, I wait, bowl of half-eaten chips close, gaze riveted to the screen, the staccato of gunfire beating in my ears as John kicks ass and bad guys fall.

After a second or two, what I assume will happen happens.

The TV goes dark. A single line of code crawls across my screen. A prompt, the rapid flash of a curser accompanied by the sound of typing and—

"Why cannae we see her?" a deep voice with a thick Scottish accent asks. "Is the bloody thing even working?"

Someone sighs. Sounds impatient, then...

"Shut up, Ran. Let me concentrate."

"Legit question, Lev." A third guy, one whose voice I recognize instantly. Vyroth, identical twin to Cyprus (commander of the Scottish pack). "Need tae get this done under the radar—before our lasses come back."

"You mean—find out," Levin grumbles over the furious click of typing. "I cannae believe I let you talk me into this shite."

"I donnae know what yer worried about," Rannock says, voice full of gravel...and a whole lot of edge. The kind that usually ends with someone getting their head ripped off. "Priya doesn't have a dog in this fight. Yer mate willnae care if we talk tae her. Niki and Cate on the other hand—"

Levin snorts. "Have you met my mate? She has a dog in every fight."

"Journalists," Rannock mutters. "So bloody nosy."

"Necessary evil," Vyroth says. "Have you seen the list of big stories Priya's broken?"

"So she's a rockstar...whatever." The low growl echoes through the line. Rannock again, sounding even more pissed off. "Lev—"

"Pulling her into this isnae a good idea."

"Donnae give me that, mon." A creak interrupts the audio, making me picture Vyroth leaning back in his chair. "You wanna talk tae her just as much as we do."

Rannock grunts. "Mayhap even more."

"You wouldn't be hacking into her feed if you didn't," Vyroth says, sounding so reasonable Levin curses, making me want to laugh.

Lifting my feet off the ottoman, I push out of my slouch instead. As I sit up straighter, I listen to more rapid-fire typing and the shuffling of feet. Chair springs squeak. One of the guys mutters something under his breath. Static blows across the computer screen. The video feed flickers before dragon warriors appear in living color.

Multiple pairs of eyes narrow on me. One set ice blue, the second hard, metallic bronze, the third mismatched, one violet iris, the other electric blue.

I stared at the trio.

All three scowl back at me.

Planting his hand on the desktop, Rannock moves closer.

I cut him off just as he's about to speak. "I know why you're calling, but I don't have anything yet."

Levin's dark blond brows pop up. "Nothing?"

"At all?" Vyroth asks.

Bronze shimmer fires in Rannock's eyes. "Where is he?"

"I don't know," I say, then start talking fast when he glares at me. "I know as much as you do. Biscayne's still hiding out in the Grampian Mountain Range. He's cleared out of the Fae village and taken Tamarack and his followers with him. I told you before—when I get a line on Legion, you'll be the first to know. Though…"

I pause.

"What?" Levin growls.

"I may have a lead. There's a woman in Biscayne's encampment who—"

"Bloody hell." Vyroth sighs and looks skyward. "There's always a lass."

Ignoring him, I sail past the interruption. "If I can get a message to her, she may be able to help."

"Is she in trouble?" Vyroth asks.

Levin throws his packmate an incredulous look. "Of course, she's in trouble, mon. In way over her head if she's tangled up with the likes of Biscayne and Legion."

"We need her name, Scribe," Rannock says, calling me by the handle all dragon warriors use when talking to me.

"Ran—"

"Name." Planting his forearm on the desktop, Levin shoves Rannock aside and leans in, drilling me with icy eyes from over three thousand miles away. "As soon as you have it, Scribe…aye?"

I nod.

He continues, "Check yer inbox. I'm sending you a link. Any new information, you send it through tae me. No delays. We need tae know where Biscayne sleeps."

Vyroth grunts. "And donnae forget about Grizgunn."

"I haven't," I say. "The Danes are in the mix—collaborating with Legion now."

"Bloody hell, lass," Rannock grumbles. "You should've led with that intel."

I frown. "I'm telling you now."

Rannock scowls.

Levin shakes his head.

Lips twitching, Vyroth reaches for the keyboard. "Later, Scribe."

"Later," I mutter. "Say hi to the girls and Lapier for me."

I get three chin lifts a second before Vyroth hits a key. My screen goes dark. The red light on my laptop blinks off. The movie starts playing again, and I'm left sitting in my writing lair, wondering about the mysterious woman embedded inside the enemy camp and how she could be the key to everything as John Wick wreaks havoc in Japan.

Read more about the Scottish dragon-warriors in book 1 of the Dragonfury Scotland Series, FURY OF A HIGHLAND DRAGON.
Buy your copy here.

SLOAN AND THE NIGHT OWL

I've never been one for midnight runs, but lately, restlessness has been chasing me. It happens sometimes, so every once in a while, I find my feet tapping down the front steps and hitting the street. Not my favorite nighttime activity, but the walk to the diner isn't the worst one either. Mel's Place. A haven with good coffee and chocolate cake when the writing's not going well, and I can't sleep.

The restlessness is Kruger's fault.

He's being a pain in the butt, doing what he always does, withholding what I need to get rolling. Experience tells me it won't last. Kruger will cave and begin to trust me...eventually. But until then, I need chocolate, coffee, and lots of fresh air.

As I turn the corner, the gloom deepens. Streetlights flicker. Night air thins as the heavy chill thickens. A prickling sensation gathers along my spine, delivering a sense of something.

Something I know all too well.

Shoving my hands into my jacket pockets, I slice between two parked cars and cross the street. There's an alley on my left. A bus stop to my right. Mel's neon sign flashes pink up ahead. I keep my pace steady, boot soles striking concrete, knowing I'm being watched, but not caring. If whoever's out there wants to talk, he'll—

"You should've left my chair out of it."

The deep voice rolls out of the alleyway. Prickles intensify as I stop and gaze into the darkness. Cloaked in shadows, a man looms large, shoulder propped against the brick wall in front of a dumpster, dark gaze shimmering green.

I tip my chin. "Sloan."

"Scribe," he says in greeting.

"You're out early tonight."

"Gotta bone to pick."

My eyebrow twitches. "Really?"

"You shouldn't have—"

"People needed to know."

"Not that much."

I sigh. "We've been over this already."

"We need to go over it again."

"Sloan," I murmur. "I'm in the inner circle. You and B put me there. Time to stop being pissed about it."

With a grunt, he pushes away from the wall. The heavy beat of footfalls echo as he walks out of the alley into the light. The urge to retreat claws through me. A natural reaction to Sloan. The guy is immense, and not just because he's nearly seven feet tall. Everything about him screams dangerous —the intensity of his expression, the lethal vibe he throws off like pheromones, the hard glint in his eyes.

He stops five feet away.

I tense, but manage to hold my ground.

He scowls at me. "Some things are private."

"Not that."

His eyes narrow.

I suffer the immediate need to explain. "You needed a push. I gave you one, now you're talking about it, giving it to Theo, healing in ways you've always needed. Your son was beautiful, Sloan. Simeon deserves better than to be kept a secret."

"He was everything."

"Yes."

"*Everything*."

"I know."

"And now, I have Theodora and Violet." Dipping his head, he leans in, getting closer, the intensity in his gaze making my chest ache.

Fighting to stay even, I nod.

"You gave them to me."

"They were always meant to be yours."

He shakes his head. "*You* did that."

"Sloan—"

"Thank you, *Kazmea*," he murmurs, using the nickname Bastian gave me.

I take a shaky breath. He's been through so much. Too much. Has suffered more loss than any Dragonkind warrior should, so...

"There's no need. The kind of guy you are, you deserve the best. All the—"

Footfalls beat across pavement. "We done with the love-in yet?"

"Frigging hell," Sloan grumbles, glaring at someone behind me. "You mind, brother?"

"Nope." Deep voice. Eastern European accent. Unrepentant attitude.

I glance over my shoulder. "Hey, Ven. How's it going?"

Shoulder-length hair in a messy man-bun, Venom steps onto the curb. Feet planted beside the bus stop, he meets my gaze with his ruby red one. "I knocked up Evie."

My lips curve. "So you're feeling good."

He grins. "Yeah."

"Congrats, man," I say, pleased for him. "I know how big that is for you."

Venom tips his chin. "Wick says hey."

I snort. "No, he doesn't. Wick hasn't talked to me in months."

"He's too busy banging J. J." A wicked gleam in his eyes, Venom shrugs. "No room for anything else but killing rogues."

Sloan chuckles.

Expression moving from teasing to alert, he glances at Sloan. "Time to fly out, man."

"Yup," Sloan says, treating me to a chin lift. "Later."

"Later," I return, and then they're gone.

One moment there, suddenly absent, leaving me alone on the street a block from Mel's, wondering when Sloan or one of the other Nightfury warriors will visit me next.

BLACK DIAMOND LAIR
ALL HALLOWED EVE

Mac set the chainsaw down in the middle of the antique tabletop. The bump of steel against wood joined the crackle in the fireplace, echoing through the room as the jagged teeth of the blade bumped into a bowl of cheezies. Set up for the regular Saturday afternoon poker game, the table overflowed with the usual...an endless supply of artery clogging junk food. Not that any of his brothers-in-arms cared about potential cardiovascular implosions. Humans might've, but not them. Their dragon DNA worked too fast for that, healing them from the inside out, before any degenerative damage could be done.

A huge bonus for all the dragon-warriors, considering the battles fought night after night with a rogue faction of their kind.

Shoving a candy dish aside, Mac repositioned the chainsaw, going for maximum centerpiece effect, then glanced toward the end of the table. Seated at the head of the mahogany monstrosity,

Wick's gaze met his. The warrior raised a brow, his silent inquiry more effective than words.

"Leatherface...Texas Chainsaw Massacre." Wick threw him a baffled look. Mac's mouth curved. It figured. Trust the most violent warrior among them to be cinematically challenged. "Never seen the movie?"

Hands shuffling a newly opened deck, Wick shook his head.

"You need to get out more." Fingering his blood splattered dress shirt, Mac loosened his tie, tugging the tattered fabric of his plaid vest to one side. "Where's your costume?"

"Halloween is for pansies."

Mac snorted. Classic Wick, direct and to the point, much like a steel-toed boot to the head. No surprise there. Neither was the fact their resident sociopath never deviated from his usual attire in-side the lair—ripped jeans, faded, beat-to-hell T-shirts, and combat boots. So Halloween and dressing up? Nah, not really Wick's style.

"Who's a pansy?" Heavy footfalls playing second fiddle to the disembodied voice, the ques-tion drifted in from through the open archway.

"You are," Mac said, trash-talking, knowing who was about to enter the dining room.

Right on cue, Venom came into view. Dipping his head to avoid getting his noggin whacked by the timber-beam lintel, the big male crossed the threshold. Mac blinked. Holy God, the guy's face looked as though it had been put through a meat grinder. "What the hell are you supposed to be?"

"Road kill."

"Niiice," Mac said, reluctant admiration in his tone.

Wick rolled his eyes.

Venom grinned, and grabbing a chair back, sat in his usual spot halfway down the table.

Moments later, the other Nightfury warriors filed in. Ahead of the pack, dressed as Optimus Prime from the Transformers, Sloan threw a package of red licorice onto the tabletop. Plastic crinkled as the candy slid to a halt beside the pile of poker chips, and Mac got a load of Bastian. He frowned, taking stock his commander's get-up. Circa Pirates of the Caribbean, B tilted his Captain Jack Sparrow hat in a rakish manner and scrubbed a hand along his whiskered jaw.

"Myst likes pirates," B murmured, a wicked gleam in his coal-lined eyes.

Mac laughed, liking his commander's game plan. A costume for the Halloween themed poker game with the guarantee of getting lucky with his female later on. Damned good strategy.

Knuckle-bumping B on the fly-by, Mac tipped his chin, greeting his mentor as the Scot entered the fray.

"Who's ready tae get their arse kicked?" Forge asked, adjusting the codpiece on his Scottish troll costume. The wart on his nose quivered in protest. "'Tis all over but the crying, lads."

"Arrogant prick." Bringing up the rear, Rikar shoved the Friday the 13th hockey mask to the top of his head. Ice blue eyes glittering, he pointed a machete in Forge's direction. "Get ready to lose, Scot."

"Give over, you wanker," Forge said. "No one beats me at Texas hold 'em."

"Then you've never played me."

The quiet assertion slithered through the room, soft accompaniment to the hissing shift of shuffling cards. All eyes turned to far end of the table, following the deep voice. Golden gaze aglow, Wick sat with a bent-to-shit halo askew on his dark head. As far as costumes went, it wasn't much. In terms of a threat...crazy effective. Cuz one thing for certain? An angel, Wick was not.

ACKNOWLEDGMENTS

I often write short stories about the characters who visit my imagination. I like to know who each one is—what's important to them, what they think about the world they live in, along with how they feel. As each word hits the page, I enter their sphere, gaining insights, teasing out information, painting a picture so I not only understand the person they are today, but also who they'll become in the future.

Writing these snippets has become an integral part of my creative process, helping me connect in real ways with the characters in my books. The extra stories I write have always been for me, and me alone. At least, that's what I thought, until one day, on a whim, I shared some on a blog.

The response I got from you, dear reader, made it clear you wanted more. You wanted the inside track. All of the tiny details of Dragonfury life that never make it into the books. And so, I give you Fury of Affliction, a compilation of some of the stories I've written about the Nightfury dragon warriors and the brutal world they inhabit. I hope each one not only entertains you, but also draws you deeper into the mayhem of my imagination.

A huge thanks to Tanya Crosby at Oliver Heber Books. Your patience and understanding helped me weather some dark days. I love working with you. I'm so grateful to be part of your crew.

To Katherine Ward – thank you for digging in and helping me put this collection together. It was a bit of a scramble, but we made it!

To my girls — you're the best. Words cannot convey how much you mean to me. I couldn't do what I love without you having my back.

A NOTE FROM THE AUTHOR

Thank you for reading **Fury of Affliction**. If you enjoyed it, please help others find my books so they can enjoy them too.

Recommend it: Please help other readers find this book by recommending it to friends, in readers' groups, and on discussion boards.

Review it: Reviews really help authors find the right audience. If you have a minute, please let others know what you liked about **Fury of Affliction** on Amazon, Goodreads, or wherever you buy your books.

Follow me on Facebook, Instagram, and Bookbub to get all the latest news.

Sign up for my Newsletter and get exclusive VIP giveaways, freebies, and sales throughout the year.

Book updates can be found at www.
CoreeneCallahan.com

Thanks again for taking the time to read my books!
You make it all possible.

ALSO BY COREENE CALLAHAN

The Mirror Kingdom Chronicles

The House of Starlight and Shadow

Rise of the Slayer

The Clash of Two Queens

Dragonfury Series

Fury of Fire

Fury of Ice

Fury of Seduction

Fury of Desire

Fury of Obsession

Fury of Surrender

Fury of Destruction

Fury of Aggression

Fury of Affliction

Dragonfury Scotland

Fury of a Highland Dragon

Fury of Shadows

Fury of Denial

Fury of Persuasion

Fury of Isolation

Fury of Frustration

Fury of Misfortune

Dragonfury Bad Boy Shifter Series

Fury of Fate

Fury of Conviction

Circle of Seven Series

Knight Awakened

Knight Avenged

Warriors of the Realm Series

Warrior's Revenge

ABOUT THE AUTHOR

Coreene Callahan is the bestselling author of the Dragonfury novels and Circle of Seven series, in which she combines her love of romance and adventure with her passion for history. After graduating with honors in psychology and taking a detour to work in interior design, Coreene returned to her first love: writing. Her debut novel, *Fury of Fire*, was a finalist in the New Jersey Romance Writers Golden Leaf Contest in two categories: Best First Book and Best Paranormal. She lives in Canada with her family, a spirited Anatolian Shepherd, and her wild imaginary world.